TROUBLES
IN THE
COLONY

DAVE ROE

For Niall and Jean

Dave and Geraldine

Nan and Pop

the Dianes

Roe, Dave

Troubles in the Colony / Dave Roe / wikidPress / 2017

ISBN: 978-0-9947856-2-6

Thanks:

Glen Tilley, for the élan; the writers and native satirists of St. John's, notably Edward Lloyd Riche, Gerry Porter and others seated at the Tannenbaum table; Jen Allford, for creating new worlds; Joan Sullivan, for the kind edit; Jack Fitzgerald, for his research into the true story of Treasure Island ; Bud (Austin) Greene for the impish wonder; Tony Hancock for the long view; Charles Peet for the ~tude; Scott W. Goudie for sharing the art of printmaking; my brother Ian for being a great guy; Ray Fennelly, a man of vision; the genuine Jere Mossier; the real Niall Burnett ; Nick Scott, for the blessing and email; Peter Brooks, for being excellent; Hanno Ehses + Horst Deppe, people who know, know; Phyllis Artiss for failing me in a university creative writing course; Greg Dawson, for the friendship; Ira Bridger for the mentorship; Loyola and the lads in St. Bon's – it's all a laugh; The Ship, when it was sailed by Newfoundland artistic pioneers, mad creators who blazed many a trail others now stroll; and everyone who puts up a smile at this troubled life.

Special Thanks to Doctors and Palliative Care nurses, everywhere.

Troubles in the Colony

Published by wikidPress

St. John's, Newfoundland

2017

Print Edition

First Printing

05.27.2017

www.wikidpress.com/DaveRoe

Design, publication: wikidPress

Contents

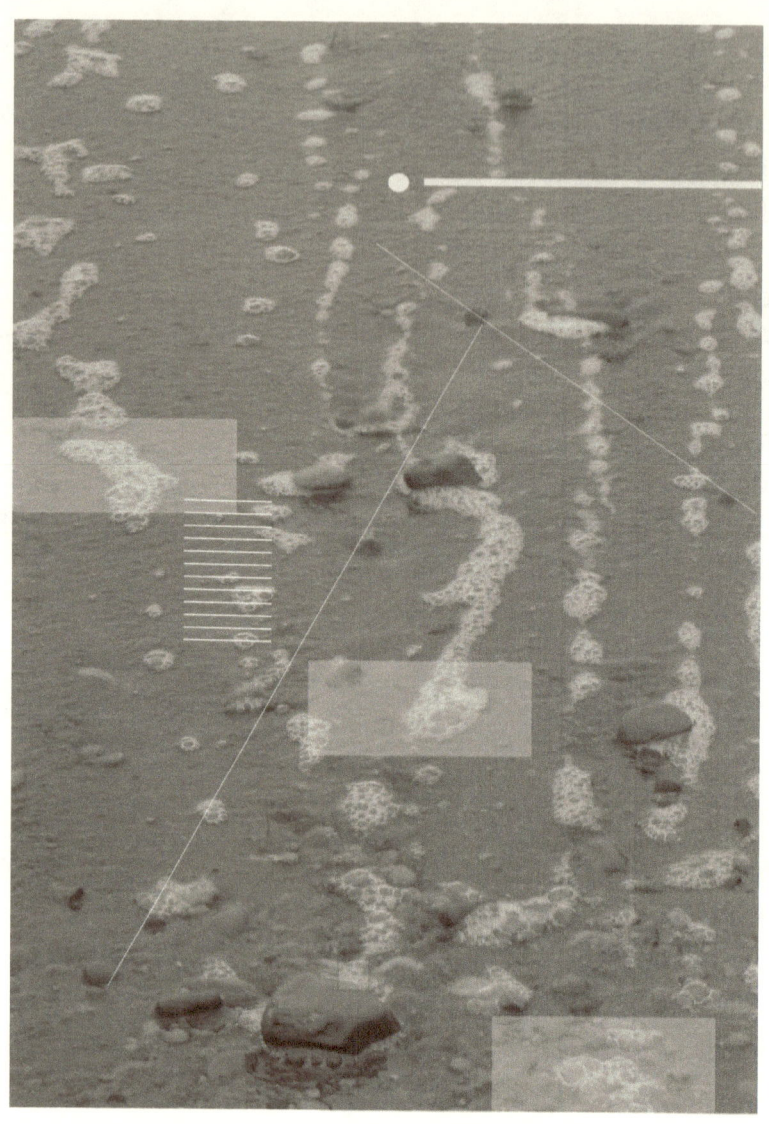

Reconstructed image - Jean's phone

My Report

[This collection is the best contiguous and consistent set of stories we have from people who witnessed the Event. The stories have been woven together using a wide range of conventional and cutting edge technologies.]

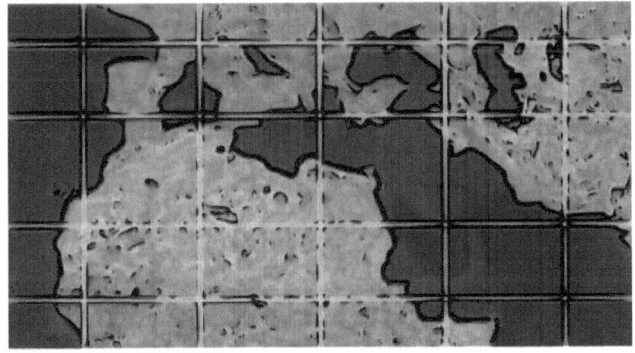

Exhibit **A**, Scan of Event location

Other variants, though valid and valuable in their own right, do not have the Event marked. Our observations absolutely show the geographical consequences, so our own narrative most be rooted to this recreation.

The people of this time appear to have had a peace like no other, yet they were always searching for more. We may conclude the pursuit of peace is peace.

These people lived in a place called Newfoundland, which is the higher part of the Atlantic plain, in and around the old city of St. John's. Contemporary scholarship has suggested it was a hard place to live. It appears to have been a colony, a deeply troubled colony.

They were fond of mirrors, dogs, and their hair. They do not appear to have been scared. They were very curious. The answers they accepted as a group, were widely different from individual principles. They were innocent, by their own accord. It just happened.

The Institute of Narrative Reconstruction

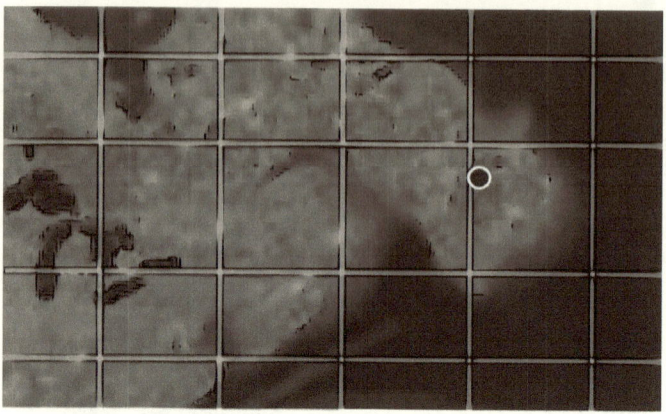

Exhibit **B**, Scan of Evidence location

Meanings are still being mined from the accounts. The logic is difficult. The practical application of the knowledge banked from this exploration may be of value for future generations. The claim framing the search for meaning as a waste of cycles, is not supported by the Institute.

The finding of early digital material in the 'Livingstone Homestead' has provided core physical elements to this story, and imprints from DNA have presented several possible narratives, the following being the most likely.

Extracting narratives from DNA has finally been machine enabled. The process reverse engineers the experience of a human on psychotropic drugs; the explosions within their nerve cells releasing primitive, universal narratives. Machine enabled narrative extraction works in reverse; able to read the shadow of people's lives as their experiences were imprinted on their nervous system. This results in a lower use of symbolism - less dragons, more descriptions of meals.

Many stories extracted to date have been incomprehensible, non-inspiring or just too hideous to record. This report is only made possible with the collaboration of dedicated biological storybuilders, natural pattern reconstructionists, and nuclear narrators. So my sincere thanks and appreciation for the practitioners in the field of Narrative Extraction must be noted. The high turnover rate is something we need to

b

address if we want to continue to mine stories and have this view into the past. It is hoped this folio will offer encouragement to the dedicated men, women, and machines who make it all possible; and provide incentive to the young to contribute to the upgrades when needed.

The captures are in near-chronological order, which is the best construct offered through analysis. When placed in a strict chronological sequence the narratives break down, sometimes coming to a complete end, often getting shredded into personal inner dialogue.

Significant events, here called 'Defining Moments', have been distributed across the collection. These have worked as keystones for the algorithms and projected data to seed against. Lloyd Porter developed the critical nurturing patterns while capturing refracted radio waves to reconstruct the soundscapes of the past. His input and direction were paramount in adopting the breadcrumb method to DNA Narrative Extraction. In many ways, this folio is his work as well as the Institute's.

Project Lead: NF7717044

The Institute of Narrative Reconstruction

Index

Mass, 71, 74, 79, 81, 238
Mineral, 225
Molten, 58
Motion, 73
Obstacle, 75
Outcrop, 2, 3, 7
Passageway, 189
Rockface, 56, 57, 75
Scree, 74, 189
Seacliff, 77
Slab, 58, 85, 94
Slate, 253
Small
    Beach rocks, 71
    Throwing, 58, k
Structure, 85
Subsurface, 131
    Molten, k
Surface, 71, 74, 249
    Slope, 71
Type of music, 2
Uprising, 56
Vantage point, 249
Weapon, 222
Ships
    RMS Newfoundland, 121, 126
    SS Brunswick, 121, 122, 126
Species
    Extinct
        Neanderthal, 63
The Geraldine Mary School of
    Names, 164
The Picture of Dorian Grey, 127
The Top Men of the Oriente, 131
Totally Made Up
    BirdShite Island, 142
    doda, 207
    Spanlish Channel, 142
Treasure Island, E, 127, 146, 197,
    207
Water
    Analysis, 110
    Ancient Sea, 56, 58
    Atlantic Ocean, 4, 80, 96, 129,
    190
    Bathing, 112, 193, 194

Beach, 71, 74, 76, 77
Bog, 96
Ceremonial, 224
Ceremonial use, 105
Coastal, 131
Disturbed, 143
Drinking, 88, 117, 138, 267
Drinking water - Commercial,
    198
Dynamics, 79, 80
Earth core, 269
Element, 144, 190, 198, 202
English Channel, 54
Environment, 138
Environmental, 140
From the tap, 20, 21, 47
Harbour, 67
Horizon, 77
Indian Ocean, l
Industrial use, 86
Inlet, 80
Lake, 54, 56, 160
    Quidi Vidi, 134, 159
Life force, 110, 207
Local, 110
Municipal, 198
Nautical, 129, 141, 142
North Sea, 54
Nuisance, 79
Ocean spray, 78
Pictoral, 1
Pond, 238, 249
Rain, 194
Religious, 235
Riparian zone, 11
Small inlet, 76
Sound, 71, 77
Splash, 143
Spring, 234, 245
Structure, 77
Surface, 80, 142, 143, 144, 145
Symbolic, 118
Territorial, 130
Tidal, 77, 81
Tide marks, 76
Tourism, 109

Images

Time for a Change

[This is the beginning, for the purposes of this report. If removed, the narratives flow towards the favelas of Brazil, an audience captivated by live streamed theatre from downtown St. John's.]

I N THE MOVING IMAGE VERSION, the opening would be a close cropped shot of a poster, possibly on screen long enough for the audience to read. The poster features large text, "Trouble in the Colonies", with a photograph of an 18th century British soldier merged with a smaller image of two women, overlooking water. The poster would be blocked by coloured blurs - brilliant, saturated swaths of garment and skin. Torsos would swipe across the screen, left to right, visible from the shoulders down to the hipbones. The torsos would eventually crowd out the poster. The view would pull back to show people lined up, handing tickets to a young woman in a redcoat. Her uniform would be ill-fitting, and the tall black cap tilted back. Most of the people in the line are middle aged. Many are older.

Another shot, affording a wider view, shows another young woman in full redcoat uniform and full discount makeup checking a text message on a mobile phone, oblivious to the people traipsing past her.

Pulling back, we see people moving along the side of a hill overlooking the harbour of the city of St. John's. It is a spectacular backdrop. There is an area of grass marked off. People find a place to sit.

Below them, in a small flatter area of the hill, sits a rough table and small flagpole, featuring a limp Union Jack. A large outcrop of rock lies at the back, to the left looking down. Behind the table, 20 feet back, sits another large boulder, large enough for someone to hide behind. Another rock, slightly smaller, sits a grocery aisle length further down to the right, in a meadow featuring tall grasses and a few gnarly fir trees.

Holding on the scene long enough for the audience to put the pieces together - that there are a bunch of folks sitting on the side of a hill presumably to watch a summer production of 18th century British soldiers - the next scene would go back to the female ticket taker we met earlier. Perhaps she is one of the people we will get to know more about. We already know it is some kind of modern production, because there are females wearing period British soldier uniforms. This would not have happened in the 18th century. We can also get a sense the young women see this all as a simple summer job.

The ticket-taker gathers the tickets in a pile, removes a small handful of the stubs, and stuffs them through the front of her uniform somewhere in the binding of her bra. She checks her nails, painted red with a small black star on each nail. Individually the nails each have a letter on them. On the left hand fingers are the letters "F-R-E-E," on the right - "N-F-L-D".

"NFLD" has been forgotten, a peculiar kind of freedom.

Back to the scene on the hill.

On the far right, we see a figure moving along a path through the meadow far down the hill. A woman, wearing a long flowing dress with a billowy top, carrying a woven bag over one shoulder, approaches the perched audience. She is humming a period Flemish tune, with a New Jersey arena rock beat.

A stray dog wanders on the edge of the meadow.

Fifty feet from the woman, a British soldier stands up from behind a rock and yells "Halt!" The woman stops. The soldier shoots. The woman falls to the ground, yelling "I'm dead!"

The British soldier steps through the tall grass towards the fallen woman. The soldier is clumsy. His hat appears oversized. The bottom pieces of a hockey helmet can be seen where the military hat finishes.

The dog is gone.

Now the wave of the story rolls back slightly, after first lick.

Two actors are standing behind the large rock outcrop. One, dressed in a ranking military outfit, addresses the other, outfitted as a colonial planter.

"We have two extra shows, for two weeks, in two weeks, in Placentia," he says. "Tuesdays and Thursday"

"Placentia! Is there money for gas? Frig."

"We can talk about it," the elder man says.

Heard through the wind someone yells "Halt!"

A young woman crouching behind another rock outcrop beyond the set table strikes a match and lights a firecracker. In no time it explodes. "I'm dead!" is shouted in the distance.

"That's my cue," the elder man says to the planter.

He walks out towards the table, holding a sizable book under his left arm. He has trouble with his hat in the wind.

He pats the book. He addresses the audience.

"Great seas petition great governance."

The firecracker woman bangs on a snare drum. The younger man comes out from behind the rock and saunters towards the senior soldier.

"Greetings Captain Cook. Fair winds today!"

"Not a Captain yet," the senior actor says. "I'm still a Lieutenant."

The planter continues towards the table. "Fair winds!"

"Easterly on the shore yesterday. Seaward today. The mail has finally arrived." The actor opens the book. It is an old phone book, with walnut mactac on the covers. It was on loan from the Legion.

He holds up a folded sheet of paper. "We have our report."

Back over to the first soldier we met. Closer, you can definitely see he is wearing a hockey helmet under his hat. He is standing over the woman. She is lying down in deep grass.

"Are you French or English?" the soldier asks the woman, directly, in his non-acting voice.

"English."

"English. So I'm French"

"No, you are English. This is the start of the play. I'm English. You shot me by mistake."

"Right," the soldier says.

The woman props herself up on an elbow. "Now you have to pick me up and carry me to the table."

"Right."

The young planter stands beside the Lieutenant.

"Good to have word from across the water. Good to know we have not been forgotten."

"They would not forget us, and our troubles."

The planter nods his head. "Troubles. Plenty of trouble."

4

He holds out his hands and wags his chin at the book. The Lieutenant hands him the book by instinct. The planter snatches it and makes a turn, showing the Lieutenant his back.

The elder Lieutenant says under his breath, "What are you doing?"

"I'm not going to Placentia unless I gets gas money," the planter whispers. The Lieutenant steps around to the front of the planter.

"Let me read the letter," the older actor plays to the audience. "The report about what to do about the Troubles."

"Beg your leave, good sir," the younger actor says, turning towards the figures on the meadow. "This map to our stockpile may get in the wrong hands." He opens the book and removes the folded paper.

In the moving image archive, there would be an insert of the piece of paper, unfolded. 'Lines of the play, w-o by hand' is how the shot would be catalogued. There would be an early discussion by the editors as to whether the audience could make out the script. The insert shot would remain in the film throughout the editing process, until it was tagged unnecessary and deleted before the final cut. It would later be re-added for cable distribution, as it helped pad before the commercials.

All versions were available digitally, for free.

"This map is in our memory. It should not get in the hands of the enemy," the planter says.

He hands the book back to the Lieutenant. He makes a show of tearing the paper with the cheat notes in two. "We have enough troubles."

Tossing the bits of paper into the air, the planter asks the Lieutenant, "What says the letter?"

Not missing a beat, the elder actor opens the old phone book and randomly tears out a page, POWER-POWER. He hands the sheet to his colleague.

"Why don't you read it, Planter Ryan? I misplaced my eyeglass." In mock fright he adds, "Skraelings perhaps!!"

A small titter of laughter bubbles out of the audience.

The first British soldier struggles up the hill, carrying the woman he shot. His hat has slipped sideways, revealing more of his hockey helmet.

He screeches, "The French. The French!" Reaching the table, he drops the woman, hard.

"Trouble!" the Lieutenant says beneath his breath.

"Troubles. The French! The French!" the helmeted soldier echoes.

The actors were clearly lost. They had needed to read the letter to set the stage for what passed as a costumed plot of judgement and punishment. The soldier had arrived earlier than expected.

Due to his brain injury they were all thankful he showed up at all. In rehearsal he usually barked "The English! The English!" The elder actor suggested he be called Private Toffee to help him remember which side he was on. But he had to change costume and dress as a French soldier in the second act. It seemed beyond the man's operational capacity to see the bigger picture, or at least his place in it.

He even had a hard time playing dead in the third act, at least in rehearsal. This was the first performance.

"The letter. The letter!" the Lieutenant demanded. "Planter Ryan, read the letter forthwith."

The planter threw the book on the table and turned his back towards the assembly.

6

The impact of the book on the table was simply too much. The table twisted slowly, skewing sideways like a folding card table, and collapsed.

"Jesus H Christ," Fiona screamed as she landed.

The planter, Tony, we will probably get to surnames later on, ran over to her side and laughed a little.

"We have to find something else, Tony," she said. "This is not what I had in mind for summer season."

The firecracker woman behind the rock, stood up to see what was on the go. She played a paradiddle on the snare.

"She lives. She lives. A miracle in the colony!" the Lieutenant yelled.

"I wish I were dead," the actress muttered into the ground.

"You are dead," the helmeted soldier confides. "I shot you."

Fiona laughed. "Jesus, Billy. You're some help."

"You tell me to 'stay still' when I'm dead," Billy adds.

Fade to black.

Found on storage – Livingstone Homestead

Created from residue on coins found in metal box

A Proposal

[Further work is being done on this cluster. Focused accounts from the people at this capture are distributed.]

Chick Flix

Street in Georgetown. From Luke's Camera

E ARLY EVENING, on the back porch of a stale watermelon-coloured house in Georgetown, Luke and Mark look through the kitchen window at a striking young blonde wearing a green wrapdress. The young woman looks like a French classical painting, rendered with incandescent lighting.

There is a party happening at the house, or waiting to happen, depending on your experience with parties.

"Swedish," Luke gestures towards her with his beer.

"No. I'd say Saskatchewan. One of those prairie Germans."

"She looks Swedish to me. Prairie girls do not dress like that. They'll all boots and jeans."

"Who's she here with?"

9

"She came with the chick flick crowd," says Luke. "That's natural blond. She can't be prairie."

Mark lights up a cigarette. "You have a point."

Image extracted from Luke's phone

THE PARTY, an informal mixer, was hosted by Phil, who recently decided he was going to try to make a living in the world of drum circles. Some said he was a brave hero, a seer of truth, an alternative evangelist. Those close to Phil knew he had a difficult time getting out of bed before noon, and was generally too vain to work for others.

Bud wasn't planning on staying too long. He probably should have gone home after the earlier wine and cheese, but Phil's was on the way, and you never know who might show up.

Bud poured himself a lemonade. He looked around the kitchen. Christopher was talking with that gal who smelled like she was off food, and another gaunt, adult emergency. There was a striking blonde, hopefully a nurse. The hair stylist, with unbelievably simple hair, was staring into space, perhaps calculating. In the corner, a couple of English as a Second Language teachers were chatting, perchance about Korea. The permanently bored marxist baker was rubbing his eyes, looking tired. More of the movie crowd should be arriving soon, so Bud decided to saunter towards the living area, to assess if there was good seating, in case he decided to stay.

He passed by two lads. They looked a bit rough around the edges.

"Who is the ugly chick?" one asked.

"Which one?" the other responded.

He paused for bit, waiting for the doorway to clear, and got a look from a St. John's purebred.

Her hair, the colour of mottled hay, veiled her face. Her face, worn smooth, matched her lithesome body. Bud felt he had been greeted by a jaguar at a watering hole. He hesitated, his neck tingling. He could feel thistles being drawn across his back, neither tickling nor stinging, promising to do both.

Two couples were on either side of him; one in the kitchen, the other in the hallway.

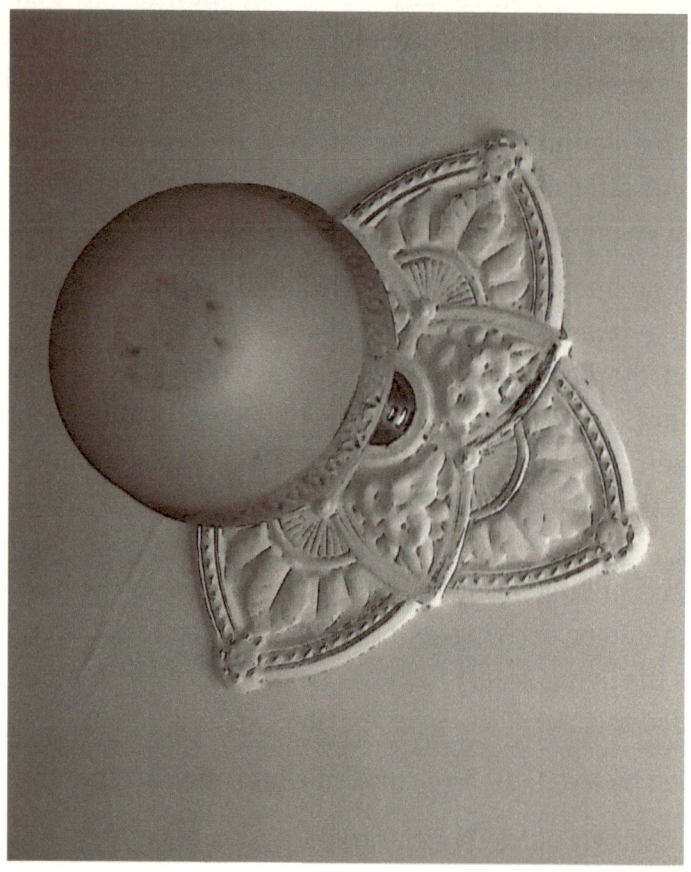

Image found on portable memory - Livingstone Homestead

A YOUNG BEARDED MAN - trying his best to look like a slightly older looking man, one older than the version of himself without a beard - obviously had one of those Irish Butler phones, because he was talking into it.

Talking to his phone seemed to be an important part of a conversation he was having with a young woman with impossibly long, twisted, dark hair.

"Finbar," the young bearded man said, talking over his shoulder, rather than to the phone directly in his hand.

"Right here, sir. You are looking in the wrong direction."

"Command," the young bearded man stated, as if he was talking to a dog. The phone vibrated in his hand, and played a low descending note.

"Wait three seconds before responding after name Finbar is stated, once."

"But sir,..."

"Raise draft Command up to level 3."

"Done" the phone acknowledged. "Invoked."

"Finbar, find - World championships, gold medal winners, pizza, St. John's"

The phone snapped back. "Seventeen Gold Medals. Do you want me to read the businesses - Question - winners, by proximity?"

"Save," the young bearded man said. "Winners would be an appropriate synonym, in context," he added.

"I knew it was more than ten," the young woman said.

"Saved," the phone promised.

"Christopher," the phone chimed. "Proximity alert. There is a young woman nearby...," the phone beeped, "...who matches your search queries from earlier today."

"Finbar !" the young man said.

The woman stepped away from the young man. He twitched at his beard.

"Lookin me up now were ya, ducky," the young woman said.

"Your photos. I saw some of your photos online and it piqued my interest."

The young woman bit her lip. Thinking.

The young man's phoned beeped a sound mimicking 'EXCUSE ME.' It continued, "She has been looking you up as well, sir. I am communicating with her assistant, Bridgette."

The young woman started to rummage through her purse.

"Sir, she has downloaded four pictures of you, as recently as today."

"It's one of those Quebec phones," the young woman said. "It's a bit slutty like that."

"Pardon? What's that about Quebec?" asked another young woman, wearing a light scarf.

"Nothing, really," the woman with the photos said.

"Thought I heard something. I am visiting from Montreal."

"Where in Montreal?" asked another bearded young man.

"Ontario."

"Want to hear a joke?"

"Sure. Is it a Newfie joke?"

"This Newfie was rowing a boat...," the young man started. He made a rowing motion.

"Was he wearing the hat?"

"Yes. He was wearing the hat. Where was I?"

"A Newfie. Rowing a boat. Wearing the hat."

"Yes. There was this Newfie rowing a boat, singing. Singing,

> 'Oh, Jack was every inch a sailor,
> Five and twenty years a whaler;' "

Fingers flash.

"Two Martians show up. One says 'A human. Let's experiment.' "

"'Let's", the other says.

"I'll take away a quarter of his brain, and we'll see what happens."

"Good," the other Martian said.

"Good," said the young woman from Ontario, Montreal.

"The Martian zaps the newfie in the boat, removing half his brain. The newfie is a bit shaken up. Then he picks up the oars and starts singing '*Jack was every inch a sailor.*' Again.

'Interesting,' says one Martian. No change. With half a brain. I'll zap the other half of his brain, see what happens.

He zaps the Newfie in the boat."

"Now he has no brain," say Ontario.

"The man in the boat drops the oars. Like before. Then he picks them up and starts singing.

> '*Frère Jacques, frère Jacques,*
> *Dormez-vous ? Dormez-vous ?*' "

The woman from Ontario, Montreal was concussed by the joke. Speechless.

"You must know some jokes," the young man said.

"Merde," the woman said.

"Suit yourself. Most jokes are 1, 2, 3. I was doing you a favour, keeping it to 2."

DEEPER IN THE HALLWAY, another couple chatted. Bud was all ears.

"If we do two, three weeks - we break even. And a month?? Too much of a risk," Tony summarizes.

"But we are alive. I don't know how many more 'Troubles' I can handle," Fiona says.

"As bad as it is, with actors wearing helmets, actors showing up drunk, actors sending text messages during a goddamn performance, its money in the bank. There's too much of a risk trying to put on our own show."

"I need something, Tony. Something to get me through this. This isn't theatre, its day camp. Day camp for acting retards." She let that sink in.

"A scenic picnic."

"With costumes."

"For senior citizens," she finished.

Tony looked up at Fiona, and Bud, the guy looking in.

"To put on a show, it's a minimum two week run. A 100 seats a night, if they are all sold - as if that ever happens - 100 times 10, so a 1000. At 20 bucks a ticket, clear, that's $20,000."

Fiona nods, she knows the impossible math.

"Add three weeks rehearsal with five actors, a bit of marketing, and pay the tech, there's probably three grand tops for each actor."

"That's fantastic!" Fiona says. "Six hundred bucks a week. Each."

"But only sell half the tickets, give comps to everyone you know to get bums in seats, still have to pay tech and get some posters, everyone gets to split $5,000. That's 200 bucks a week."

"Just covers the aspirin and wine."

"It's too much of a risk," Tony said.

Bud moved closer. "The only way to do it is do it for a month with a sold out house every night. And for every bum in a seat, there also has to be someone in their lap - holding a small person, somehow."

Bud positioned himself square across the hallway.

"And I can sell those tickets for you."

A young bearded man, who looks like he hasn't seen a mirror in six weeks, passes between Bud and the actors.

Fiona asks, "How long?"

"Three days. All the seats will be sold three times, every night, for a month. One hundred and five seats, right?

Tony nodded. This was interesting.

"Three hundred seats a show, five shows a week. Four weeks. 6,000 ticket sales. 20 bucks a ticket clear. One hundred and twenty thousand dollars. In three days."

Fiona is taken a back. "The boy knows his numbers. We can do matinees while we are at it."

Tony smiles. "What show will we have to do? "

Bud leans back against the far wall. "I'd suggest a review. Something that changes. I can see us doing 15 shows a week. Need an ensemble."

Fiona leans forward.

"Rough numbers. Let's shoot for $100,000. If we can do that we can do $300,000 easy."

"My cut on $120,000 is 20%, so that leaves $96,000 to pay the bills, which we can do for $50,000. No problem. That gives us about $50,000 after a month, and we decide the next project…"

Fiona, "Who's 'we'?"

Bud smiles. "The Downtown Creative Collective. I am the president. You are the Secretary/Treasurer and construction lad here is the operations manager."

"Vice-President, Operations and Programming," stated Tony.

Bud smiles again. Too easy. He reaches a hand out to each of them. "Deal!?"

Fiona and Tony shake hands with Bud.

A young aspiring director, Colleen, hopped into the hallway and watched them seal their agreement.

"Good things happen in threes" Colleen sings. "Always!"

"And bad things never happen." Bud laughs.

"Hold it mister. Let me show you my bruises," Fiona said.

Colleen leans in. "He'd love to see." She brushes through the basket of forearms, on her way into the kitchen.

They each take a sip of their drink. "Are you the Bud they call Bonsai Bud?" Tony asked in a tone that was part curiosity, part accusatory. "You are aren't you?"

"Yes." Bud shifted the weight on his feet. He was arming himself to leave. In St. John's there are several unauthorized biographies of your life in circulation. There was no telling what copies Tony had been party to.

"I've heard of you. You're the dope grower," Fiona said. She stared at him. This could be a lot of mistakes.

"I hybridized a single bud weed plant which can be grown in your kitchen, like a Bonsai tree. You just have to keep it," Bud snipped, "trimmed."

"I've seen those! They are brilliant!!" Tony beamed. "Any here?"

"'Fraid not," Bud said. "Not the plants. But if you ask some of my customers, such as Luke and Mark, they may have been tending."

"Bonus." Tony nodded.

"Give me three full days. Prepare to be real busy." Bud gave a wide smile and pivoted towards the great rooms.

Fiona shook her head. "Stoner."

Tony shook his head in disagreement. "He hardly smokes, I heard. He's just real smart."

"And kinda cute," Fiona said, in agreement. "What do we have to lose?"

"Do we keep the guy with the helmet?"

"Billy," Fiona filled in. "God. Yes."

"You are drinking water?" Tony said.

"Yes. I went over to Sarah's on Wednesday to watch 'Downtown Detectives' and we played 'Take-A-Shot'."

Tony shook his head. "What's that?" He knew the television show, but not the game.

"Every time Buddy grabs a gun or a cel phone you have to take a shot of rum."

"Ugly."

"I passed out before the cartoon bears tried to sell me toilet paper. Twenty-six minutes in I blacked out. I have hugged my own toilet more than my friends the past few days."

"Water. Good choice then. Need to hydrate."

Extracted from found cloth - Livingstone Homestead

LUKE AND MARK had come in the kitchen from the back door and capped a beer from the fridge. The blond went out into the back yard. They followed.

"It's just three chords."

"Not if you play it right."

"The playing is in the wild, not in the changes. But how you recognize the changes."

"Silver," Luke concluded. *'Silver'* is what he said when he more or less agreed with you. *'Gold'* when he was totally on board, and *'Bronze'* when he thought you had a point, but a weak one. Other than that it was *'Didn't place'*.

The lads stopped on the edge of the back porch. Luke nodded to the blonde, chatting with Colleen. Luke had heard of Colleen. She had her own glow around her.

"Excuse me," Mark said to the blond. "Were you at the market next to the Dutch consulate last week?"

"The Norwegian Consulate you mean."

"Right. The Norwegian one."

"No. That wasn't me," she laughed.

Mark felt a tad trapped in his own snare. "I always get them mixed up."

"Sandra was just telling me she has a twin, an exact twin!" Colleen informed Mark.

"It was probably her. She works at the consulate."

"World peace!" Luke cheered.

"Love and Peace." Mark raised his glass for a toast.

"Love and Peace," they all chimed.

"And you have a twin. The world keeps on giving," Mark slipped in before taking a sip.

"What brings you lads here? You spent half the evening in the back yard," Sandra asked.

"Outside is good," Luke responded. "More of it the better."

"We're musicians. And we are working on some projects. Some productions." Mark cracked his neck slightly.

"Such as...," Colleen asked.

"'Rogue Rovers' is the one we want to do," Luke volunteered. "We are just getting mobilized, looking for a tube."

Mark smirked a bit. He didn't want to jump into the 'Rogue Rovers' just yet. This could be a real 'bonk your head' in Luke's terms.

"What's Rogue Rovers? Encampment with the British ground troops?" Sandra asks.

"It's about wild dogs near urban areas. Dogs given up by their owners and set free just outsides of cities. They go feral in a few weeks," Luke pitched.

Mark said, "There's a human side as well. Stories about the heartbreak of owners having to give up their dog, and their reactions to seeing them go wild. You own a dog?"

"Yes. A small Labrador. My sister Sophie has a Newfoundland. That's why our family decided to move here. I am from Cincinnati. We got those dogs, fell in love them and my parents decided one day...", she turned towards Colleen, "my parents decided we should all move here. It's great."

"Welcome," Luke said. Another raised glass. Another toast.

"Norway? Cincinnati?"

"My great grandfather, five fathers ago, moved to America, from Norway, the Faroe Islands. The Faroe Islands now flies the Danish flag."

"That was a while ago, a bit of an issue between the Danes and the Norwegians, I am sensing," Mark stated. "Where are the Faroes?"

"In between Norway, Scotland and Iceland."

"Brutal," Luke said. "When did the Danes get it from the Norwegians?"

"1814, or 1948. Depends," Sandra answered.

"And you still pining over it?" Mark asked.

"Never give up your independence. 'The world is built by those willing to march' my Farfar used to say. My grandfather."

Sandra looked at Luke and Mark, assessing their resolve. "You Newfoundlanders have given up on your sovereignty. And proudly, I see."

"We prefer Canadian shoe leather over rubber boots pressing down on our heads." Luke laughed. He pulled Mark's hoodie over his head and mimicked a hockey fight.

"So this is St. John's," the blond said. "I can tell it's not Oslo."

"Good things happen in Newfoundland and Labrador." Colleen added as the boys horsed around.

A young lad turned, making room for the ruckus. He looked like several members of his immediate family frequent taverns featuring no natural light.

"Likes fights," he mumbled to himself.

Reconstructed from a variety of sources, compilation

From "Logy Bay" area, buried refuse

Bait and Switch

I T IS CUTE that the owner of the hockey team kept an office at the arena, just for show mainly, and perhaps for a bit of privacy, but really there is no need. The guy is hardly around. Name a place on the planet and he has been there in the past two years. He travels constantly, mostly on other people's dimes. In the exercise of bread and circuses, the office was a part of the main tent.

Bud managed to get a meet on short notice. "10 minutes tops," he said to the secretary in the office.

Bud only had to wait 10 minutes himself before the bossman came out and offered his hand. "Will Daniels. Proud owner of the Frosties. Pleasure to meet you."

Bud reached out his hand, preparing to have it possibly crushed. He gave a slight squeeze - a millisecond. Will Daniels did the same, just a tinch longer.

"Please come into my office," Daniels offered.

Bud followed quickly as Will made a small 'coffee' gesture to the secretary. It was probably code for 'make sure this guy isn't here longer than 10 minutes' for all Bud knew.

Will sat behind his desk, a position designed for photo ops. The wall behind was a collage of banners, plaques, hats, and framed photos. Bud was impressed. On first glance the collection did not appear vainglorious; these items were mostly about the team.

"Bud Livingstone, President of the Downtown Creative Collective " Bud said as soon as he sat down.

"How can I help you Bud?"

"The Downtown Creative Collective is launching a community-based show. We have unique opportunities for sponsorship which will provide amazing exposure for those willing to participate." Bud looked above Will Daniels, to the pictures on the wall, then returned to Will. "And I wanted to start with your team, because of your incredible success and wonderful public image."

Will smiled. He nodded. "Participate," he echoed.

"We are offering sponsors the opportunity to pay it forward, to help the arts, to help the citizens of the city. For the run of our show we are offering sponsors the opportunity to cover all the tickets for audience groups."

Will scrinched his face a bit. This was a new pitch.

"So I'd like to offer the Frosties the chance to pay for all the tickets of people under 18 who come to the show, or you can buy seats for all the seniors who attend."

"Interesting," Will responded. "Is that it?"

"There will be plenty of publicity. You are the first to be given this choice," Bud said.

"There is always No", Will said.

"Yes. I did not come here to discuss No. It's an interesting offer. Your head says go for the kids, they will remember that you helped them for the rest of their lives. The heart says go for the seniors, cause everyone loves seniors and wants to help."

"Good point" Will responded. He liked how the kid was playing the game.

"If you pick the seniors, and people know you could have picked the kids - word will get out - you will be perceived as having a big heart. Pick the youth, and folks think you might be ignoring the seniors."

Will laughed a bit.

"And if you say no, and word gets out, well - is it really worth the trouble?"

Will nodded instinctively. "Is this blackmail?" He loosened his tie for effect.

"No is the answer there. This is an opportunity to visibly support the community that supports the hockey team," Bud answered. "It's a gift to yourself."

Bud looked at his watch. Two minutes left.

"And I need a cheque by the end of the day, to reserve a block of tickets. The show starts in a month, features every actor and creative type in the A1C. Even if they wanted to, this crowd will never raise their voice against you again, that has to be worth $15,000, just for the peace of mind. This comes with great community stewardship points."

Will tapped his pen on the desk. "Bud. Bud Livingstone. You Leonard's son?"

"Yes sir." Will Daniels and Bud's father were neighbours in Logy Bay. "I figure I have two minutes left, Mr. Daniels."

Will Daniels smiled and looked out the window, over the harbour of St. John's. His eyes went soft.

"Leonard and Noelle's son. I have all the time in the world for Noelle's son," Will said. "An extraordinary woman. You will have what you are looking for."

"Debbie !" Will called out. "Bring in the chequebook. This man has a schedule. We don't want to take any more of his time!"

Better than expected, Bud mused. Gold.

Fifteen minutes later he was able to get a good visitor parking spot at the foot of the Peckham Insurance Building. A few minutes more, he was on the fourth floor and introducing himself to the receptionist "Bud Livingstone to see Emily Canning." In another eight minutes he was seated at a conference table with Emily, Director of Community Initiatives, some blond in Marketing, and a young well-suited man who looked like he must be one of the Peckhams, learning the business. If he had married in, his shoes would've have been well worn, Bud conjectured.

Emily nodded and offered Bud her card. "Some introductions. I am Emily Canning, Director of Community Initiatives."

"Kieran Peckham. I work with community relations," the man offered, positioning his card on the table.

"Tiff Oppenday, Marketing" the blond held the card upright on the table before placing it in the line of business cards before Bud.

Bud leaned forward, reached out his right hand and placed his fingers on the three business cards. He paused for a second. His fingers lined the cards up. He touched Kieran's card with his middle finger and leaned back in his chair.

"Bud Livingstone. I am President of the Downtown Creative Collective. I won't take more than 10 minutes of your time. Thank you for meeting with me on such short notice."

He leaned forward and spread out his hands, as if he was holding a ball.

"We are staging a show which will basically involve almost every sector and arts type in the A1C, a show which we are offering selected sponsors a unique opportunity to participate in."

Emily gestured she was going to say something; Peckham jumped in.

"Bud, our community relations department, and our family's foundation, work with the artistic community quite a bit. I am sure you must know this."

"I am aware of how you help the artists," Bud nodded. "This offer is how you can help the general community."

"How can you help us help the community?" Emily said.

"We are offering Peckham Insurance the opportunity to prepay for all the tickets of certain sectors of the population."

"What did you have in mind?" asked Emily.

"During our run, six weeks, Peckham Insurance can offer free seats to young people. Future customers who do not have enough access to the vibrant arts experience in this great city, where Peckham Insurance has it head office."

The marketing lady stirred in her seat.

"The other option is members of our Armed Forces and their families. Our Armed Forces face extreme risk so we can live safely."

Bud's hands fanned out, handing the ball to those on the other side of the table. Kieran, already far back in his chair, shifted his weight.

Emily summarized "You want us to buy, or guarantee, tickets of a certain audience group. For a period of six weeks of shows."

Bud nodded.

Kieran countered, "We have our own summer camp in Salmonier, and every year two unfortunate children from the city are given a free attendance."

Bud did not bother to smirk. He laid the fingers of his left hand on the edge of the table. "The head says help the children. The heart says help the armed forces," Bud directed at Kieran. He looked towards Emily. She would make the real decision he figured. "If people know you had the choice between kids and war vets, and you choose war vets, people will truly remember this generosity for a long time."

"They died for our country," Kieran said.

"We donate plenty to the war poppies. And we help the Memorial Day parade every year," the marketing lady said.

"How?" Bud asked.

"We supply all the parade participants with free coffee, and donuts."

Bud placed the fingers of his right hand on the table, then turned both hands on their side, controlling a space between them.

"If people hear you could choose between the war vets and the kids, and you refused, and this allowed Continental Agents to have the sponsorship, then that is your decision."

The blond leaned forward "Have you approached Continental yet?"

"No. But I can be there in 20 minutes. They follow my social feed, apparently."

Tiff shot Kieran a quick, nearly imperceptible, dirty look. There must have been a history of emails, meetings, and budget reviews on 'social media' which perhaps did not go her way.

"How much are you looking for?" Emily asked. She wanted to get to the point.

"$12,000 will reserve the seats, and help us publicize your sponsorship."

"That's a lot of war vets," Kieran observed.

"We may offer valet parking for the amputees and the soldiers in wheel chairs," Bud said. "We thought it would be a good service."

Tiff was there to protect Kieran. "This show, when does it start? Tell us more about it."

"It's a cabaret. A review. A collection of timely skits and theater arts. We will bring in dancers, musicians, magicians - people will love it." He quickly looked over his shoulder. "This is the hottest craze in Ireland at the moment," Bud made up on the spot. He knew Kieran was bit of an eirophile.

"Interesting. Family show. For amputees," Kieran said.

"Most certainty," Bud responded, thinking to himself: Family show if your family fridge has a dozen in it and a medicine cabinet with plenty of pills.

"I need a cheque by the end of the day. After lunch preferably. Our social media team is ready to start making the announcements.

"Will Continental be offered the kids, if we go for the vets?" Tiff asked.

Bud's hand reached into his inside pocket.

"No. We will not approach Continental at all, of course." He pulled out a card and a cell phone.

"Why bring them into this, when we can keep it local."

Emily said, "I think we have enough information to make a decision Mr. Livingstone."

There was a beat and Bud beamed. "I see there is quite a selection of magazines downstairs." He put the cell phone back and handed a business card to Tiff. "My cell number. You can text me if you like."

"We had 378 settlements last year on cases linked to people texting," Tiff said, being on message.

"We tell people to turn off their phones before the show. We can add 'Please don't text and drive', if you like."

"Perfect," Kieran said. He stood up, and attended to the door. "We will talk to you soon."

"Cheers," Bud said, and he left.

Magnetic resonance – Canadian Shield

Defining Moments – Tony

Comin from behind

TONY'S SKATE LANDED solid on the ice. Jumping over the boards, he pushed himself immediately into the play, lifting the blade of the winger's stick and stealing the puck. He passed it short to Richards, pressed a stride, and received a quick pass back, taking their center out of the play. Williams called out from the opposite wing "Gus! Gus!" Tony heard his teammate beckon using his elementary nickname. The stadium boomed with people shouting encouragement and derision. Tony shifted the puck to his backhand and pivoted his center of balance to deliver a hard pass. He snapped the puck at Williams, past a lone defenceman between the two wings. The defenceman turned his skate to slow his backward motion and started to fall between the two. Williams passed the puck back. Tony was 25 feet in front of the goalie.

There's a 1:42 left in 5th period of the 5th game of the City High School Championships. Second period of overtime in the deciding game. We are back in time a bit, back to Tony's defining moment.

Coach Murphy hardly used Tony in the playoffs. Tony was great for the team, great for the practices, looked great in pictures, and he had a car. But Coach Murphy thought Tony lacked the sense of hunger of his teammates.

Tony had a couple of shifts in the second period, and one pivotal shift in the third. Tony scored the tying goal during that shift, a quick deflection in front of the net from a soft shot from the point.

A few minutes earlier there had been a fight on the ice, rare in overtime playoff hockey. It was a bloody fight among 16-year-old males. Six players were penalized, three from each team.

When the crowd stopped yelling and screaming, booing and jostling, the blue smoke in the stadium cleared enough to show the time clock. Everyone was aware it was the 5th and final game in the series. The clock showed the score to be 5-5, in the 5th period, with 5:55 remaining in the game. Collectively the crowd stopped and took it in; then they went absolutely nuts.

Primal.

In the game of life, the Collegians had won hands down. This reality was being understood by the players on the Celts. The Collegians, primarily of the protestant High Anglican faith, but with plenty of Lutherans, Baptists, Methodists, Presbyterians, Uniteds, and Salvation Army, had the distribution of wealth and opportunity pretty much in their hands.

The Collegians were known as Prods. The Celts were Micks. The Prods lived in the new Jerusalem. The Micks tended the city walls.

The Prods had better teeth. Drove finer cars. Lived in nicer houses. Took more vacations. Had cabins in prime locations. They were healthier. They lived longer. They had more lucrative jobs.

They were the judges, the lawyers, and the doctors. They were the senior civil servants, the ambassadors. They owned distribution companies for products made elsewhere. They controlled what was sold out of this place. They controlled the police, the army, and city hall.

This was all a consequence of their birth, and which religion their family followed.

This country followed the general rule that the head of the monarchy had to be a High Anglican. The head of the monarchy was head of the High Protestant faith, and was also the symbolic head of the legal framework for the whole.

In places where they ruled, the High Anglicans gave the primary means of local distribution to other High Anglicans, and assorted Protestants.

The people who ran the government, who ran the banks, who interpreted the laws and supplied the hospital facilities, the people who commanded the military, who imported the goods, who distributed the goods people needed, they all went to St. Andrews Collegiate.

Not only did this happen in St. John's, Newfoundland, but virtually in every commanded post of British influence. There was always a St. Andrew's. Newfoundland was just the first colony in the British Empire.

In a sporting event the odds were a little bit fairer. Both sides had a chance and the Celts had the most to lose, as this was one of the few opportunities they had to win.

So here was Tony, 25 feet in front of the net, with a defenceman in an uncontrolled spiral to the ice a few feet behind him, and a goalie ahead. Tony shot the puck at the goalie, at the spot below his blocker and above the heavy pads on his legs, knowing with the cross-crease movement the goalie would not be able to close the gap.

The puck shot past the goalie, towards the net, hitting the post and ricocheting hard up the ice off the boards. Tony turned in time to see a Collegian knock down the flying puck, bounce it off the boards to get by the lone Celt defenceman, and deke the goalie to shovel the puck in an open net.

Tony's world went dark. He failed to win. He made the tie giving his team another chance but he failed to finish it off. His status of hero was lost and the almost-hero missed chance was made worse by the fact he was the last Celt to touch the puck before the Collegians scored.

His father and mother were supportive. His younger brother, Jim, watched him carefully. Tony spent a lot of time alone. His mates thought they might have to live through the moment from Tony's point of view and avoided him.

His parents had recently rescued a dog from the pound. The pet could not have arrived at a better time in Tony's life.

Two weeks after the game Tony sat down in his room and wrote what started out to be a poem. He simplified it into a song, called *Comin' from Behind*. He took it to the band teacher, Mr. Peet, who arranged for a few students to do a recording. Mr. Peet overlaid tracks of horns and choruses and sent the tape off to an associate in New York. The tape sat in a library for many years. Then it sat in a garage after the music company Mr. Peet's associate worked for folded under the digital storm.

The son of Mr. Peet's associate found the tape and uploaded it to a web site of found audio files.

Then, one day in Oklahoma, a college DJ gave it a spin during a college football game. Tony's life would change once again, resurrected.

Exercise. Write an inspirational song.

Write a song about being in a situation where your opponent has the upper hand, and you are inspired to rise to the challenge and beat them. You are coming from behind.

An example of a song is found in this collection.

This is a good learning opportunity.

Comin' From Behind

From trail debris by Livingstone Homestead

Five Per Cent

[The analysis focused on many of the following characters as being required for the main focal area of the report. Interestingly enough, this analysis utilizes 'Livingstone Points.']

L EONARD WAS NOT SURE what to make of the email. It was from this fella who said he had a blog and asked for his phone number to have a quick chat. Leonard hoped it was something about the business, but usually requests from the various types of scribes came with some sort of explanation. He tapped out a short response with the area code and number and pressed the Send button, launching his phone number into a sea of numbers, arriving at a numbered port, somewhere.

He had just opened another message when a notice of the reply from Niall Burnett windowed on his computer, giving what seemed to be the total body of the message in the small coloured box – "Thanks. Ring!"

The phone rang. Leonard picked it up. "Antitocia - Leonard Livingstone."

"Niall Burnett here, sir. What is Antitoxia, Mr Livingstone?"

Leonard did not bother to correct the mispronunciation, as he wasn't sure it was worth the effort at this point.

"My business."

"Sounds interesting."

"How can I help you Mr. Burnett?"

"I am calling to ask you about your nomination."

"Which nomination?"

"For the Ramaksenkhar Prize, Mr. Livingstone."

"Fill me in Mr. Burnett, please."

"You have been nominated for the Gandhi Institute's Ramaksenkhar Prize in Economics. Has the nominating committee not called you?"

"No. Why would I get nominated for a prize in economics Mr Burnett? I run a detox center."

"I would imagine you do it very well Mr Livingstone. Where do you live?"

"Who are you? What is this about? This does not sound right."

"Bear with me Mr Livingstone. This is not a scam. Did you write a paper called 'Watch the Five Percent' while at Memorial University of Newfoundland?"

He pronounced it fully, completely, as 'New-found-land' with a heavy weight of the second syllable. It was the mistake of someone who had not yet been corrected to the familiar 'New-fun-land', usually in the easily memorable phrase 'Understand Newfoundland.'

"Yes I did. If you are stealing my identity, you have a lot of information. Who are you?"

"I write a blog called *'Shifting Sands'*. It's about how jobs in Western economies are being transferred to South Asia, so I watch the area quite closely. Your nomination has caused quite a stir. Do you have any comment?"

"No. I have no idea what you are talking about. I run a spa, a place where people come to get healthy. I know nothing about this 'Raka-whatever' prize, I try to avoid western economies as much as I can, and India is some place on the other side of the planet that I have little contact with."

"Your paper, the paper you wrote in university, has changed economic theory Mr Livingstone. A man named Sujith Baku has been claiming it as his own and the Institute was preparing to give him the prize for economics. But there have been revelations that his work is based on your paper Mr. Livingstone, so the committee has decided to give you the prize, rightfully so."

"I don't get this. You're saying some paper I wrote as a 20- year-old kid is getting me a prize in Economics from India? That's whacked."

"I am quite serious, Mr. Livingstone. Mr. Baku is on suicide watch since all this came out. It turns out a student of his in the 1990's recalled seeing your paper on his desk, and he did some digging. It seems Mr. Baku's economic dissertations have all been based on a paper you wrote. You said you were 20 when you wrote it?"

"Yes. And I think I only got a B+ for the paper as I recall."

"Your paper was digitized in 1995, and was referenced in an early tele-conference of social economic policy the same year, put on by, one second, the Extended Media Center at Memorial University. A 'Mr Scott' made the presentation. Was he your professor?"

"Yes. He was. He told me I was not fit to be an economist and should pursue the humanities. I remember the conversation, because it was not one conversation - he mentioned it to me several times - openly in class. It was a bit of a joke. I would raise my hand to ask a question and he would say 'What query does the fiction writer have today? Let us let him entertain us,' he would say."

"Your paper has had a radical effect on economic policies, scientific studies, brand marketing, and military campaigns for the past five years, Mr. Livingstone. It was called the Baku Cluster, but now people are calling it the Livingstone Point."

"What are you talking about?"

"You identified that to have better success in preparing for the future, people who have access to data should watch the groups, the trends, which pass the five percent barrier, for they will become the next big thing. I am summarizing, of course. Excuse me. It is the latest trend in cancer research. You are credited, Mr Livingstone, of creating the foundation for effective Smart Data."

"And Scott said I was crazy."

"He used it the basis for a presentation he did on economic policy, and applied it to two disparate situations - Predicting Trends in Urban Drug Use and Civic Livery Management. Mr Baku did the same thing in India in 1997, claiming the approach as his own."

"I see."

"Mr Livingstone. Your theory has become a game changer, so to speak. It is compared to Game Theory. It is programmed into how trading is done on all stock markets Mr Livingstone. In fact someday your theories may be blamed for a collapse in the market."

"That's rich. I give people blueberry tarts and baths of fresh cranberries, barely making ends meet, and some guy from cyberworld phones me up and tells me something I wrote when I was scraggly 20-year-old may be the cause of the collapse of the stock market. I've some strange days Mr Burnett, but I have to tell you this certainly ranks."

"Excuse me Mr Livingstone, but this is a bigger, fresher story that I thought it was. I was simply going to write a piece on the collapse of the India School - that's the popular name for the Indian economists who have been using your approach for the past number of years. The revelation that Mr Baku is a bit of a fraud, that's the story I was going after. I had no idea you had no idea about any of this."

"It's news to me. I knew Scott was a fraud. So did his wife."

"I could get this to the Guardian, the London Times, the Herald, as a paid piece Mr. Livingstone. But I would need more of your time."

"I have plenty of time, Mr, Burnett."

"I can fly out right away. I'd like to do this in person. Where are you located Mr Livingstone? New Jersey"

"Newfoundland. Logy Bay. Where are you coming from?"

"Durham, United Kingdom."

"Good luck."

"And can I ask that you not speak to others about this Mr Livingstone. It will give me a better chance on selling the story, if I have the story first. You understand."

"Not really. But I don't have enough time to chat with strangers on the phone. Trust me, I won't chat with anyone else."

"Thank you very much, Mr Livingstone. And, excuse me, I meant to offer my congratulations earlier on winning this prestigious prize."

"What goes with the prize, beside phone calls from strangers?"

"Close to a million dollars, and there may be a likeness on a piece of currency, or perhaps a stamp, I will look it up. You can look it up yourself Mr Livingstone."

"I have waited this long. I can wait some more."

"I will send my details via email once they are arranged Mr Livingstone. Once again, thank you very much for taking my call. I look forward to meeting you."

With that, the phone returned to dial tone. Leonard looked at the phone in his hand, and shook his head.

Bud's car showed up in the lane and stopped in front of the house. There was a young woman in the passenger seat. Bud motioned her to wait, jumped out of the car and came up the stairs to the kitchen/office.

"Who's the pretty young thing?" Leonard asked.

"Colleen. She wanted to see the place. I told her to wait a minute. I'll give her a quick tour."

"I see. Aren't you going to ask me what's new?"

"Sure Dad. I wanted to find out how many you have coming in first. Need to do a wee bit of planning."

"There's eight. Germans. Book editors and designers. They are double booked." Double booked meaning they were going to stay twice as long as people generally stayed at Antitocia.

"Perfect. Most of the arrangements have been made."

"Sure. Sounds good. I will have to get something at the get go to calm them down. They could be a twittery bunch."

"Tea and scones should do it, like always. The saunas are ready, and stoked." Bud went over to the window and signalled for Colleen to come in the building.

"Germans. A dozen. All at once. I'll need a vacation."

Bud looked around the main office slash kitchen area. It looked like he was trying to assess if there was anything new in the environment, or anything missing.

Colleen paused at the threshold of the door, and slowly positioned herself inside the room.

"Colleen, I'd like you to meet my father, Leonard. Dad, Colleen."

"Nice to meet you. This is the famous Antitocia Spa! Home of Logy Fresh! I always wanted to come here."

"You look like a wind of good promises, as my father used to say," Leonard said.

"So, what's new Dad, besides the approaching invasion?"

"My likeness may be soon on a stamp. Or a piece of currency. Should find out the next couple of days."

Bud straightened out his back and walked to the cupboard, retrieving a few glasses. "And a Most Wanted poster too I suppose."

"Careful. That too perhaps. If the New York Stock Exchange should fail, they are setting it up to blame it all on me."

"You'll have to excuse my father, Colleen. Usually he serves mushroom-laced earthy teas to visitors in this house of healing. Perhaps this morning he has been sampling his own medicine." He made a motion with the glass, from Colleen to the tap on the sink. "I just love the water here. It's the best."

Colleen nodded, accepting the offer. As Bud ran the tap she commented "How exciting! The stamp I mean, not the stock exchange thing."

"Some guy from England just phoned me. Said I won a prestigious prize in economics from some crowd in India. Comes with a million dollars. He is flying in here the next couple of days to interview me for the world's press."

"Sounds like a scam dad. Don't send him any money."

Colleen pulled out her phone and started tapping.

Bud took a few mouthfuls of water, refilled the glass and handed it to his father. "You need this more than I do."

"Is it the Ram-ak-sen-kar Prize?" Colleen asked.

"Yes. That's the one. Something I wrote in university has had an impact they tell me."

Bud sat on the couch, placing the glasses on a small table to the side. "Let's see."

"Some guy is on suicide watch," Colleen said.

"It's true then. This chap wasn't pulling my leg," Leonard said. "It's true." He raised his glass to the horizon.

Colleen sat next to Bud and showed him her phone, pushing a few buttons. Bud looked at his father. "Still, don't go writing any cheques to strangers without telling me first, okay Dad."

"I can go tell those Germans to go fuck themselves." Leonard laughed. "Sylvia quit. I'm short anyway."

"Where there's a Wilhelm there's a way," Bud said.

"I am looking for a job Mr Livingstone," Colleen proposed, adding, "I live in Logy Bay."

"I thought you looked familiar. Lemonade. You had that lemonade stand. By the bridge."

"Yes sir. My sister and I had that for years. It was so much fun!"

Bud now had Colleen's phone in his hands, scrolling and tapping.

"This sort of looks legit Dad. Who called you?"

"Some blogger from England. Burnett is his name."

"What did you say in your paper?"

"It's the five per cent thing. I've told it to you a number of times."

"Really. Watch the five per cent?"

"Yes. Apparently there's a school of economic thinking in India that does watch the five per cent and it has become quite fashionable."

Bud turned to Colleen. "Dad always used to say if you want to know what the next big thing is look around and focus on what five per cent of the people are doing. They are the innovators he said. Once they adapt something new, you'll see the use quickly grow to 20 per cent. And once it hits 20 per cent, it can easily jump to 70 or 80."

"This guy said they found this works in all kinds of situations. Cancer cells, companies on stock exchanges. I wrote it for a second year economics class. The assignment was something about post-confederation economic policies in rural Newfoundland. It seemed like a way to get students to follow the arguments being put forth at the time to close down the outports. I put together a paper that proposed all the species that were considered by-catches: the redfish, the shrimp, the turbot - could have profitable markets in their own right. There was no need to close these communities."

"There was more to it, as you told us growing up."

"Yes. It was just coincidental. People fished for cod. All these bycatches, each of them in some way or other, were about five per cent of the sales from main catch, generally. There were people willing to buy, but they needed a larger quantity. My paper was about creating new markets, not relying on a single market. Each of these bycatches could become a market, a viable economic activity all on its own."

"Good things always happen in Newfoundland, I always say," said Colleen.

"You just have to wait 35 years for the people who rob you to get caught, eh Dad!"

"If you are lucky. There's always a whole new crowd knocking on your door mummering in to rob anything you got."

Colleen piped up. "I know this guy from India. His whole family went back there for a grand tour just last year. He said he is so grateful his family came to St. John's. He said India was a shithole."

"You serious about looking for work?" Leonard asked.

"Yes."

Leonard glanced back and forth between Bud and Colleen.

"I'll hire you. Start tomorrow."

"Colleen was on the road. She needs a run into town." Bud said.

"And Bud was nice enough to offer me a ride. Funny, I was going into town for a job interview. Guess I should cancel that!" Colleen stood up, said "Excuse me," and started pecking away at her phone. She stepped outside the door.

"So when do you get this million dollars, with your likeness on the bills?" Bud asked his father.

"Probably find out tomorrow. All the candles are burning in India now I suspect."

Magnetic Resonance reconstruction, from beach rocks

The Fabric

T O KEEP THE DREAM ALIVE Fiona reached out and hit the snooze button. Her head rolled back into the feather pillow. She sunk back into her world of forms and colours, and the space between things.

The shapes in her dream fired through her optic nerve and danced in the darkness of her closed eyes. There was a grid, a structure, a fabric of points of light and dark.

The sense of space was complete, not panoramic. There was no up, no down, no left, no right - just the feeling of equanimity. No shapes, with highlights and shadows; just fields of colour. The framework breathed.

Points on the grid shimmered - circular shapes with serrated edges - into blue-green explosions of light. They floated randomly, at slightly different speeds and directions, but seemed to stay in place.

Fiona could see a shimmer of light, a change in the fabric. She catapulted her sense of self toward the movement. She could see energy move through the stuff, or rather see the pieces of fabric transform - from points to fields - their change being the light itself, her own light. Points became spinning platelets - some dissolving into fields, seemingly disappearing. The fields, the immediate creation of space, collapsed back to a point after the light had passed, in a slightly different location.

The points became a dense intersection. Some of the dark points switched to lines of energy, and collapsed back, moved by the effort. Expanding points were repelling from other expanding points, in a binary dance.

Some of the dark items, in yet a more concentrated collection, expanded and collapsed en masse, pushing other clumps of material away. At times their contraction resulted in their outward disappearance, but they bounced back in a slightly different part of the larger orbit. This elastic layer eventually formed a skin around a larger, denser, central grouping, a host of points stuck in the exploding phase of the cycle.

Fiona could see a plastic progression of changing features, she understood as light, fold through the fabric. The sequence came to the edge of the gathering and seemed to transfer itself through the grouping. She could see that each of the points or fields did alter slightly, as the message was passed, but not on the same scale as the general constitution.

The continuum shuddered. The space between the points became smaller. This went on, the contraction, until all the points converged into a space that was totally black.

Larger clusters crashed into this mass and eventually the phosphenes on Fiona's eyelids disappeared. There was a beat, then a purr, and finally a blast of light, and two eyes filled her field of vision.

Fiona was staring at Rajith's cat, Moxie. Moxie was sitting on Fiona's chest. Moxie's right paw was over Fiona's face, its claw cycling Fiona's left eyelid open and closed.

Noblesse Oblige

[This cluster is from the period they called 'Late 1800s'.
Reconstructed through pattern matching of father and son pair,
supplemented with a pristine silver-print photograph.]

One-Eyed Jacks and the Man With the Axe

LEONARD LIVINGSTONE'S great grandfather was the first to settle on the island on his mother's side. On his father's side they were pirates from Northern Bay Sands. His mother's ancestor, James McGregor, came to the island as a geologist from England. He was to work on the Northern Peninsula, and the Labrador, on special assignment to the Queen's bankers.

He did report there was significant iron ore on the Labrador. 'On the Labrador' here is a literal term. The iron ore was on the ground for you to pick up. It was hell's furnace, and the devil was away for a while. The devil does not live in the heat, the devil lives in cold. Cold so absolute you would burn yourself alive to escape.

The Queen's bankers put the Labrador report on the shelf. It was good information to have.

James McGregor decided to stay in St. John's for a bit after delivering the report. He wanted a break away from Her Majesties Prospectors. He had good money to spend, and the ladies... well, the ladies were very welcoming.

He would entertain them with his tales on the coast, and many were familiar with the places and characters featured – the pious, the maniacal, the good folk, the brazen French, the scallywags. He fell in love telling the following story of his adventure preceding his journey to Newfoundland – his trip to Northern Germany, where he saw One Eyed Jacks and the Man With the Axe.

He was part of a British team invited by the Bismarck on behalf of the Prussian king Wilhelm to look at a couple of distinctly different sets of bones. As a rock prospector, it was thought he may be familiar with such sites. The rock formations were reported to be spectacular.

James McGregor was told to pack for a week. He was going to northern Germany on her majesty's request - for her German relatives - to the original homeland of the Angles, to examine the findings.

The team was given a letter, not to be read until they were on the ship out of Channel waters.

The expedition lead, Major Stanton, shared some of the details of the missive when the trade barque started slicing the blackish waters of the North Sea. The bones looked like the bones of men, but were a form of a giant - larger across, bigger heads, stronger bones.

Two sites had been found in small outcrops that looked like the top of a cave structure, 38 miles apart. James was given some rudimentary survey data to examine.

By the time the ship approached the west coast of the Jutland peninsula James presented to the group the observation the maps suggested the caves were part of a geological pleat, and could continue for another hundred miles or so in a north easterly direction.

James advocated the team examine another area, 40 miles or so from the northerly discovery, to a spot which looked like the outline of a small eye on the isometric maps. This suggested a location of a large lake, which primitive peoples like these giants would have naturally used as a gathering place and hunting ground.

The location was very near their first stop, Major Stanton commented, it looked like it may be on the very estate where they were to stay the first night, on the outskirts of Süderheistedt. They would arrive mid-afternoon and Stanton encouraged McGregor to take a stroll once settled.

"Be mindful gentlemen, not everything we find we need to share with the Germans. We are walking into a tight pass. These bones may be claimed as top English examples of superiority - these man-bears they have found - or they may be seen as forebears to Germanic might. And the Danes are only a dozen furlongs away, and who knows what they will claim. So all findings must come to me first. Tighter than a Tunisian tunny, we must be."

———◦———

A German official, Sergeant Major Friedlander, met them on the shore and straightened them out with horses. They proceeded inland to a wood, leading to a grand estate of a Junker. A representative of the Bundesrat welcomed them warmly, quickly bringing out the bitters for liquid greetings.

James went for a walk after drinks. At the gate there was a small encampment of people waiting to see their governor. Perhaps they wanted to take advantage of the covering hanging off the tall fence for the night, a rough stable.

There weren't enough people in the camp to pose any threat, if they should become unruly. But if they were agitated, you did not want to be one of their early victories. As there was a path along the wall leading to the river, he decided to walk past those waiting. He could hear sobbing.

Three young African girls were by the small well, playing a game. The compacted earth was a good play area for young children, away from the horses. They were playing Knucklebones, and breathing the familiar chant of the game in their own tongue.

James slowed to enjoy their play. One girl was about to throw the jack when a woman escalated her sob into a sudden shriek. The three girls broke their tight circle and looked past James, their foreheads touching. Each of the three girls, who looked like triplets, was missing an eye.

He took the path by a river, and soon found the opening to the oblong plateau on the map. The ground was rich, warm and generally flat. The land behind him to the east was once mostly under water. This was part of a previous coastline. Digging down the young geologist noticed the subsoil was originally pumice. This area, formerly a lake, had been filled in by a geoclasmic explosion. He found a small stream and waded to the middle, reaching down to grab handfuls of the stream bed. It was sandy, a dark loam, a few inches below was the same pea sized pumice.

He stood up and imagined a lake being showered with volcanic ash. Did the water in the lake get vaporized by the blast? Was it sudden? Was it even a lake, or perhaps a small protected valley? The valley could be rich in fossilized remains of humans and animals if there was such an event. He would keep this under his hat for now. There was a bigger prize.

The entourage left shortly after dawn and planned to reach the first site by late afternoon. There was surprising little small talk from their hosts about what they were going to see; the Germans seemed to get grimmer as they got nearer.

They finally stopped. The German host pointed at a large uprising of rock that had been to their right for the last fifteen miles or so, varying from 30 feet above the trail to 90 feet or so. Sometimes the outcrop had a sheer rockface and occasionally it had a gentle slope, enough to foster trees and shrubs. They were at a section of cliff rising about fifty feet. The rock looked like it had been broken and the sheared cross-section angled back a few degrees away from them.

"It is impossible to see the entrance," the German remarked, moving his staff in the air, seemingly outlining a series of steps. "Young hunters had wounded a deer, which was taken by wolves here. They found the opening by following the sounds of their feeding." He removed a pistol from the horse's pack. "We must keep eyes open."

A young German led the group along an animal trail parallel to the rockface for twenty yards, then he started to climb the rocks on a natural stairway. Though he was seventh in the procession, James saw the front of the line descend and disappear through an opening spiraling into the rock the width and height of a knight. The stairwell descended to an interior space the size of James' laboratory. The German stood on a small boulder and pointed his staff at a passage almost hidden in the back of the interior room.

"This is the anteroom to the place of the discovery. The passage is the same height, width and length. It is a cube of space. The floor in the entrance, and the floor in this chamber, is perfectly level. We believe these spaces were engineered by the people we have found here."

James dragged his toe along the quartz silt of the floor. It was fairly compacted.

"The inner chamber is a marvel of nature, suitable for the wonder of giants you are about to see. Torchbearers, move to the front."

The procession snaked through the cube passageway and came to a large circular space, the negative impression of a clump of sitting bread dough. The space was four times James' height. You could throw a rock across the diameter and not hit a wall opposite.

The German stood next to a tarpaulin in the middle of the chamber and pointed at James. "How could this space be so perfectly round, Mr McGregor? Was this caused by water?"

"Probably not," James responded. "Probably an eddy of molten rock." James made a circular motion with his finger towards the sky.

"Molten rock. From the earth. Rising," the German said, before repeating the same in his language for his associates.

"Here is what we found," the German said, signalling for a couple of men to remove the tarpaulin. "As it was discovered."

James saw a collection of skulls, ribcages, hipbones and legs. Two typical skulls had fallen into the chest cavity of the remains below, one resting on top of another regular sized skull. The other had fallen into a hollow, below a massive skull, with a jawbone like a bear's and a skullcap almost as large.

The gigantic skull was atop a large pile of similar skulls.

Major Stanton signalled for a helper to bring a torch down closer to the base of the pile of bones. In the light everyone could see the tangle of foot bones, mingled in with the massive shinbones of the giants. Stanton addressed the official.

"What have you done, exactly, to this discovery, Herr Scraffe?"

The German moved back and gestured towards the ground behind the group. "The young hunters tried to move the top of this tomb, and were able to pry it enough to see some skulls, which they said scared them and they left." One of the torchbearers nodded. "It took 8 strong men to move this slab." He pointed to a perfectly rectangular foot high slab of rock 7 feet by 6 feet.

"These giants seem to be below the others. At first we saw the two ordinary skulls and one of the giant skulls. We cleared away some of the dust, the dirt, and saw the other normal skull under the one of the left, at the same level as the base of the giant skull. We cleared a bit more and saw the two giant skulls beneath those. What you see are three layers of bodies, each with a male and female. The top layer appears to be humans. The next layer appears to be a female human and a giant male. Below this you can see with your eyes the skulls of two giants."

"Were there any adornments removed?" Major Stanton asked.

Herr Scraffe patted a leather bag hanging over his shoulder. "Yes." He reached into the bag and unwrapped what looked like a necklace of large bird beaks with a conch at the center as a main medallion.

"This was around the waist of the first giant. Curious codpiece."

The conch was clearly a fossilized tooth. A tooth from a giant animal.

"And on the top, in the hands of the male, we found…" he pulled out a wedge of forged iron, with a loop for a strong handle, "this axe." He needed two hands to comfortably display the item. "A superb weapon."

The axe head appeared to be unused, perhaps polished before placement in the grave. The cutting edge was encrusted with diamonds.

"A King's jewels," said Major Stanton.

There appeared to be a blanket of bones separating the layers of human figures, two rows of animal tibiae with ribcages splayed across the lattice, bound to the larger bones.

Fennelly the photographer piped up. "These appear to be bones from a bird, now extinct. The garefowl. The beaks as well."

"Geirfugl." A member of the German team nodded.

Herr Scraffe made a point of showing everyone the axe.

"We want your help to record what is here, explain this underground palace. We want to remove these bones carefully, and as you see there are two giants on the bottom. We want to keep the remains of these giants in as good existence," his English failing him. He turned to his group and stated a few orders.

"Please. Let us go back through the cube and make some plans while my men get us enough light to work properly. If your photographer can take some pictures while we make plans, for the record it would be good. "

"Fennelly's your man," Stanton said cheerily. "Spark 'er up."

From a lost phone on the barrens, Avalon Wilderness

THE GROUP MADE PLANS for two days of digging. Herr Scraffe ordered his men to begin setting up camp.

"One layer of creatures like us. One layer of a woman of our kind and a giant, and another layer of two giants – a man and a woman, adorned. What could it possibly mean?" Stanton asked his men.

James was asked to explore the area with a young German to see if there any signs of settlement.

The group dug for twelve days. They discovered the pile had gone 15 layers deep at this point, the thirteen bottom layers all being pairs of the giants. The hole had been dug a good dozen feet deep.

They uncovered great stone axes and many strands of shell jewellery amongst the bones. They built a lattice box around the stack of skeletons as they went. Fennelly had run out of photographic plates.

Their eager beginnings had changed to reticent, calculated movements. The group decided it was too risky to keep digging, fearing that the pillar of bones may fall over. There were mentions of ancient curses in many languages.

Midday on the twelfth day Major Stanton took Herr Scraffe aside.

"We have to stop digging, tad bit of danger in the hole, Herr," he started. "We need to destroy this burial ground before tongues start telling stories of their own on what's down there."

The German nodded. "I was coming to the same bearing myself."

"I suggest we ask all in the group to empty their kit. Three from our group and three from your group go in and make a mess of this, then leave," Stanton said. "We should go to the other site, and if it appears to be the same, destroy it as well."

The German agreed.

Magnetic storage, possibly Beth's

STANTON'S GROUP took the news passively. They had expected a break in the activities, but not a full stop; not instructions to destroy what they had uncovered.

"You agreed to this?" McGregor asked.

"Believe I suggested it," Stanton responded.

"Extraordinary," Fennelly said.

"These findings show a lineage of kings and queens, who were ritually sacrificed. Kings and queens of giants who accepted their fate. The last pair of what seems to be our ancestors, and the Huns ancestors, was the end of the line. It can be assumed they did not carry on with the ritual. Perhaps they killed all the giants as well."

"This is a significant discovery," Willoughby, the botanist, said shaking his head.

"They did have the best axe," James said. "The ones like us."

"Exactly. It looks like they killed the giants with that bloody axe, or ones like it. And a ritual sacrifice of their leaders ended, when the people who started the ritual ended," the Major continued.

"Great leaders accept the greatest sacrifice, to be killed," Stanton stated to the group. "This is not what we want to tell people is the tradition of the Anglo-Saxons. And our German friends see this somehow as a shameful pile of bones," Stanton explained. "Huns feel favoured to the giants, and they see it as a defeat."

"Our German hosts are quite concerned. A chap named Engels has published a book putting forth some theories on how certain groups, societies, form. It has Germany, and the Jutes, in quite a stir. This Engels has said early societies had women in charge. Old Willy Wilheim does not appreciate people not at his table, discussing the legitimacy of those at his table."

63

James McGregor, at the back of the tent, spotted one of Fennelly's photographic plates and moved it behind his kit.

"This pile of bones suggests there was a lineage of giants, each who had a limited reign. None of the bones look like they are of old kings. They must have sat on the throne for a short period - 5 to 8 years - and then they were sacrificed. Such talk would make so much steam inside the king's head his top hat would blow as high as a kite."

He turned up his lip and straightened his back, mocking the Germans. Placing his forefinger on the crown of his head he made 'pop' sound, his finger pointed to the sky - then he made a rough whistle, raising his hand, jabbing the roof of the tent.

"Besides, our queen bee wouldn't be too impressed. She likes her head on her shoulders."

James moved ahead. He turned to the group.

"They passed the killing on, the choice of life and death, to the fates. It must be when they created gods."

He turned to a young lad, Richard's man, Hickman.

"Any signs, artefacts, of god worship?"

"None," Hickman said. "It's all below the horizon."

"They stopped praising women, created Gods, and appointed themselves charter," Fennelly said. The others laughed, uncomfortably.

"I wonder what a woman would say?" James said, lightly.

"God save the Queen," Stanton commanded.

"God save the Queen," everyone replied.

From a lost phone on the barrens, Avalon Wilderness

From organics, near St. John's harbour

Defining Moments – Fiona

Terasa

WHEN FIONA WAS 15 she was a small 15. Her friend and knock around pal Terasa was two months younger and five inches taller. When they walked along the road Terasa always took the higher ground so cars could see them better.

Terasa was the neighbourhood friend. This was a new neighbourhood by St. John's standards. The people living there seemed more mixed than the inner city, only because most people were familiar with the monotone of the city centre. Anyone outside of the centre has to go there to do anything - go to school, go to work, visit a doctor, get someone out of the drunk tank - these services were all between Military Road and the waterfront.

Terasa lived half a block away. They had only known each other for 8 months. They had met each other's other friends only once. Both events were uncomfortable. There was a different humour in each bunch. Fiona's friends, well Kath mostly, were obsessed with boys. Terasa's friends took boys for granted. They were mostly youngest siblings with several older brothers and sisters. Fiona's friends were mainly the oldest child in the family, and many of them were the only child.

Harry's car pulled alongside the girls as they turned off MacDonald Drive. "Terasa - I'm going to the ladder. Wanna come?"

It was late August, the end of the discernible summer.

"I dunno. How long does it take?"

"Two, three hours. Depends."

"Depends on what?"

"The wind. The weather. It's hard to explain. You gotta see it."

"Can my friend come?" she asked.

"Yes" said Harry.

Terasa turned towards Fiona and pursed her face into a question mark while straightening her back and standing on her toes, saying "Shag it. Let's go."

The two girls jumped in the car. They were an hour away from the most important moment of their lives.

Found material, Fiona. Day trip looking for icebergs.

Binary Recovery Unit, Fogo Facility, The Institute

Found Material - Fiona; Binary Recovery Unit - Fogo Facility

THE LADDER WAS OUT OF THE CITY a ways, past half a dozen still active fishing communities. The drive took about 20 minutes down the main road, then they had to take a turn down a graded gravel road, an access for a satellite station. The maintained road went straight for 1000 feet and then took a hard left turn. Harry turned right, seemingly into the bushes, but it was a well-worn cart path. It opened up to a grassy meadow where several cars could park.

Harry's car was a Datsun. It had belonged to his Dad. His dad's friends said it was amazing a lawn mower could take a family of four out for Chinese. So his dad gave the car to Harry as a present for getting through grade 11.

There was a large blue older car parked in the tall grass. The tires were all different shades of dark grey. One front tire was a whitewall. Somehow the tire looked like it was on upside down.

They parked besides the blue car. Two boys were in the front seat. Noddin, towards the rear, the boy in the passenger seat said, "Come on down".

The three of them jumped into the back of the Impala. "This is bigger than my couch. Where's the coffee table?" Fiona said. "This boat was made before coffee was invented," said the passenger boy.

The driver lit an Export A. The smoke feathered out the window. The wind pushed it aside.

Terasa knew of the driver, Don. She had seen his friend arguing with security at roller skating. He was getting kicked out for skating against the crowd.

"Not many knows about this. We'd like to keep it that way."

"Doesn't seem busy. What are we waiting for...?"

"Don't want to rush into it. Conlon said they might make it down. Give it a few minutes. You girls good for this? "

"For what?"

"For the ladder."

"It's a trip."

"What is it?"

"A ladder, built by the Americans. During the war subs used to come and drop off supplies for the satellite station."

"It was a radar station. And they used to bring down supplies for the subs - my old man says. His uncle was in the British Navy."

"It's a bit freaky the first time, but it's worth it."

"Everything is freaky the first time," Terasa said. The girls laughed.

"But you gotta stay cool. We all go together, or don't go," said Don.

A large prop plane roared overhead. The main approach to the airport was just south of this headland.

"We should all be introduced if we are all in this together," Fiona said. The passenger was Greg. She thought his name was Craig. Fiona always had a problem with mixing up Greg and Craig. Craig seemed like a crack in a rock, Greg seemed like something you could tie a rope around. This guy was a bit cracked, but he seemed strong. Flush cheeks and a set of arms from shovelling dirt all summer in a job he had for a few months at the nursery.

"The path is just a few minutes," Don said, rushing past the formalities. He opened his door, signalling he was ready.

"Conlon en them can meet us down there, if they shows up."

They walked down an overgrown path. The salt wind was intoxicating. Fiona remembered thinking it was better and fresher than anything out of a bottle. Her grandmother said you can "taste the wind".

The cleared path sort of gave up at a large blueberry patch. They all stopped and each picked a handful, silently, like they were doing a station of the cross. There was a break in the treeline, suggesting their next waypoint.

The trees were reluctant to invest their effort in growing tall and had decided low and huddled was the best strategy for all. Here, on a clifftop washed by brackish winds, the trees grew inches from one another, building strong intertwined fingers of roots rather than reaching into the sky for a truant sun. The thin acidic soil, a mixture of fibre from their own predecessors and little else, was mainly webbing for the roots.

Ten feet into the break their feet were on rock. Twenty feet along the rock a finger of rusty iron was attached to a crag of cement.

The iron followed the slope of the rock, and was close to a foot above. At the top, where the ladder was initially attached, the lie seemed more horizontal than vertical. One side of the ladder was a bit higher off the rock, like it had come loose. It looked like a rope ladder they would throw over the sides of ships, frozen in a gust of wind, floating above the rock. The ladder disappeared down the side of the cliff.

Fiona lost her breath. It was the sound, water raking over beach rocks below. Water meeting rock created a beat with deep reverberations. The air itself was broken.

Harry instinctively stepped back.

"I'll go first, then..." Don paused, "Terasa, yourself, Harry then Greg."

Greg said "Take our time. Six or seven rungs between."

71

"There's a busted rung just down over the edge. You just have to take your time."

"It's easier coming up," Greg said, as consolation.

Don climbed on top the ladder. It looked like he was on a broken bicycle riding it backwards. He descended to the point where they could just see his head. "Get on Terasa. The broken rung is just three rungs below where I'm standing." The wind threatened to rob the sounds from his mouth before it could reach their ears.

"How long is this? You close?"

"Only about 50 feet."

Fiona had no idea how far 50 feet meant. Terasa climbed on top of the ladder. Harry started to laugh, trying to own the space around her. Fiona jumped on as soon as Terasa was on the crest.

Fiona could feel the shifting of Don's and Terasa weight through the ladder. She timed her moves to be out of beat with theirs. She looked face down at first. When she got to the point where she thought she was would just be a floating head for Harry and Greg, she realized she had only progressed a few rungs. The descent quickly started to vertical out. She stared at her hands, feeling the support below with her feet.

Fiona looked up and could see the undercarriage of Harry's frame spidering down above her. Below, Don was instructing Terasa.

"That's it. Stretch. Stay close to the ladder."

The metal was in the shade and cold. It seemed to repel Fiona's grip.

She peeked down by her shoulder past her feet. Terasa was right below her. Far below Terasa was rock, and crashing ocean waves.

"Got it. It's not that bad," Fiona said, pausing.

"I'm doing good. You?"

"Good. Wild."

Everyone was on the structure now. They all paused.

"I think this is where the broken rung is at," Fiona said.

"It's a bit tricky getting your foot down. But what's tough is not having a hand hold. Grab the sides," Terasa said from below.

The ladder started to rock a bit. Don must have been moving faster, reaching the bottom Fiona hoped.

"Wait a bit, retard," she shot up to Harry.

"Sure."

The rung was deceptive. The iron had sheared on one side, and bent down. There was no secure footing because there was no metal, just a stub; and on the other side, her foot slipped down the support, to nothing. This was the information Fiona's wandering foot feed back to her muscles.

A loud boom-crack-boom sound reset the air. Fiona traced her foot down the side till the next rung, let out her breath and shot up to Harry. "I'm past."

"Hands past?"

"No."

It was like climbing off a bunk bed, a 50 foot tilted bunk bed with sheets of granite.

Fiona could hear Terasa yelling, celebrating. The crackling of beach rocks caused by human feet grounded her on her final descent.

She had to jump off the last few feet. Don had lit another smoke. She asked him for a draw. Terasa was wide-eyed, scanning the whole situation.

The base of the ladder was still 20 feet or so above the changing level of the ocean, a floor of fallen rocks dissolving into beach rocks with two craggy walls buttressing back from the water. Smell of smashed kelp slapped through the air.

"Look at that beach. Wow." Terasa pointed across the vista. The beach was in full sun, and looked like something out of pictures of tropical beaches in Vietnam or some place, on an island off another island.

"We'll get there. First we do the cave." Don pointed to the rock face to their left. "Then we jump the crack and crawl the wall. There's another beach, better than that one. Have a fire there."

"Cave," Fiona said. "Neat."

"Bit tricky going to that second beach. Gotta come back that's all. There's a spot..." Don made some shapes with his hands, trying to describe an impasse on the rock face.

Harry jumped off the ladder to the beached rocks.

"The crack is hard enough coming back."

"I'm so glad we came," Terasa said.

Another boom-bang-boom corrected the air. "That's the crack," Don said, making a backwards karate crop motion.

Greg finished the climb carefully, using the rock as silent rungs for a foothold as he supported his body with his upper torso. His feet on the ground, he leaned against the ladder, his hands on the bottom rung.

Fiona felt like she was on the album cover of her life, going forwards and backwards at the same time. Water meets rock, wind greets sun, and birds watch fish. For a moment all was peace. Water was not smashing rock, warmed by sun. Birds were not diving for fish. Life was not eating other life. Elements were not challenging other elements.

Greg leaned on the rockface next to ladder. "You gals did fine."

Terasa straightened her shoulders, placed her hands in front as if to say "Good, coach" and bowed her head slightly. She jutted out her chin. "Wasn't so bad."

The group stood where the two cliffs converged, creating a slanted corner.

"Jesus!" Harry said, looking out over the curved cove.

This space with all its broken lines was in direct contrast to the curves of the ocean waves and ellipses of stones at the beach. It was a gentle curve from the near vertical cliffs to the near horizontal of the waves and beachrocks.

"Looks easy to get to the cave. Doesn't look bad," said Greg.

They ambled down, feet finding footing on rounder rocks slowly slaloming to a small beach.

"Could be four. Could be five."

"There, that would have been a good one" said Don, pointing at the base of the wall of rock to their left. The wave retracted showing beach rocks at the point. Greg ran down running straight towards the wave, pushing it ahead. He turned as he went around at the point, and waved. He disappeared.

"Probably got wet," Don said. "The cave is right around the point. Sometimes the rocks are low, and you hafta kind scramble up the beach rocks to get inside."

Harry pointed at the wave rising towards them. "You have to time it, follow the wave out, then you can get around the bend."

Fiona folded her arms. Don said "Next time, follow me. Terasa, Fiona then Harry."

"We'll get there." He moved down the beach. "Face the rocks. It's easier."

The wave started to pull back and lurched forward almost immediately, a wave on a wave.

Fiona turned, touching Terasa's waist. "Wild."

The double wave slurped back into the ocean, Don crouched. Fiona could feel a tap from Harry on her shoulder right behind her. The rush of adrenalin maxed her hearing, now full of the water raking back the beach rocks. Don started following the wave, slowly at first, then the undertow pulled the water back. He sprinted down. Terasa missed half a beat and Fiona almost jumped on her. Terasa made a leap, catching up with Don and Harry gave Fiona a gentle push. Don ran along the water line as beach rocks were revealed under his feet. Both Don and Terasa looked like cartoon characters going round the edge, their feet slipping on the rolling rocks. Fiona hit the point, her feet landing on the path just carved. The sea rose again and paused, ready to pounce. Harry pushed her. Terasa made a leap to get around Don, who had slipped on the rocks piled inside the cave. Fiona came to a full stop behind Don and she grasped for air. Harry landed next to her, his arm around her waist. He lifted Fiona over Don's leg.

Terasa and Greg let out a yell. The wave crashed into the cave, the volume amplified in the chamber. Fiona looked down at the water rising under her feet. Harry's eyes bulged, his feet caught in the returning water.

"Whoa" Harry yelled. He stretched his body, standing on his toes on the water.

"Sea slippers" Greg said.

The wave of water pushed a wave of sound into the cave. The sound tried to push the water back out.

Greg pointed across the water. "We won't get that far. The good beach is over there."

"Pecker Point. Almost made it one time."

"Never again."

Terasa giggled.

The beach rocks formed two platforms across the width of the cave, natural terraces. The group sat and watched the cinema of water and sky.

Fiona yelled "Wild!" above their heads, the word sucked out of the cave.

The group tried different choruses of yells and howls. At times the yells joined together, weaving a spirit on the air. Sometimes the collective noise was ripped apart by wind and water.

"Looks like the tide is coming in."

"What moon is it?"

"Three quarters."

"You have to be quicker going back."

The water swished in, licked the beach, and slid back. A large wave smashed against the point they passed, and continued to rise, rubbing the rock.

"Now," Greg said. He took two great leaps down the beach breakwater, the splashes falling before his feet. Quickly he slipped around the bend. The water rested.

Terasa tensed. Fiona stood and felt the horizontal equivalent of vertigo. The water winched back. Don put his hands on Terasa's waist and she snapped ahead. Her feet stomped on the water as she leaned around the curve. Don started to go on the outside, pausing, placing himself between the ocean and Terasa. Then the two of them were gone.

Fiona looked at Harry. He was no Don.

"We need to wait a few. You go first. Don't stop."

Water crisscrossed at their feet. The sound was colder.

Fiona tried to judge the breath of the water. "Now?"

"In two. It will rise twice, then we go."

The water crawled up the beach, and exhaled. Fiona felt Harry's hand. She took two tiny steps and stopped.

"Go!" Harry commanded, not bothering to slow behind her.

She hopped twice, but at the turn she froze. The bowl of air around the point started to fill with water. The earth tilted. In her periphery she saw a cliff with a massive rooster tail of water rocketing out to where the water always won. Something knocked the back of her calf. Harry was yelling. She grabbed at the cliff, the water rising. She looked down.

Handkerchiefs of jellyfish hovered around her knees. Fiona pumped her legs, hopelessly hoping not to step on the creatures. Her knees were no longer breaking the surface of the rising wave. The water was getting thicker, wanting her to stay.

Harry pushed her. One. Two. Three big leaps. She moved past the point, in sight of the others.

She caught a breath and walked the rest, the water staying midcalf for several steps. The jellyfish slid into the foam.

She sat, shivered, shook and stopped. Her hearing tuned back, others applauding as Harry arrived at her feet.

"Told you not to stop. You wet?"

"Had to get my f-footing," she said. "F-fucking jellyfish. No one mentioned jellyfish."

"They're little dollar jellys. Won't hurt ya," Don said.

"Creeped the living shit out of me. Then when I saw you guys and I knew I'd be okay. I saw this giant spout. What's that?"

"The crack. That's next. Easier than the cave. Better get the water outta your shoes. Tighten your laces," Don said.

He was wearing his brother's construction boots. He finger-pulled the rawhide and wrapped the cord above the ankles, like skates.

Water spilled out of the two rivet portholes at the insteps of Fiona's flats. She made the bunny ears large so the ends were short and tucked the loops under the tongue on each shoe.

She felt like the first time she crossed the street on her own, against her mother's commandment. Instinctively she checked her pockets for candy.

"How about the tide?" Terasa asked.

"Doesn't matter now. We'll be on the cliff. There's a ledge. Water might be higher in the crack."

"Either we all goes, or we don't go. So I'll go first. Then Terasa, Fiona, Harry, then Greg," Don said.

"I'm good," Terasa said. You good Fiona?"

"Finest fucking kind."

"It's easier. But it's freakier. If it freaks ya out, that's cool. Don't do nothing you don't feel comfortable with."

"Cool," Fiona said. Harry nodded.

Don stood and walked towards the scrapheap of rocks to the right, picking a path up the mound. He stopped just past the crest, now back on rooted rock, at the foot of a cliff. The others gathered around, the young girls on the peak.

"There's the crack," Harry said.

The rock face descended another seven or eight feet, then stopped, dropping. Another rock face was across a divide. Fiona could feel the water going into the large vertical crevice, the gap between the cliffs. She heard the waves disappear.

"How far does it go back?"

"Not too far. The waves sometimes... they crashes in... and if there's another... it shoots out," Greg said.

"As long as it doesn't happen on your jump." Don moved few feet down, where the rocks were wet.

Fiona looked across the gorge. There was a wall of rock leaning back from the water, an extension of the same rock face where she stood. There seemed to be a natural ledge all along the way.

She could not see the water directly below the rockface, but there was a vantage on the general behaviour of the water in the cove. You could see it pour into the inlet from the Atlantic Ocean. There was a break a ways out, just past an imaginary line between the point to their right, and where the headland might be to the left, well past the cave. Past this break, the water was in a large overflowing basin. It rolled towards shore and seemed to hit a shelf before heaving slightly before the beachhead.

Don looked up at them. "You have to put your left foot on a ledge, just here," he pointed with his foot. "Then you push yourself over. Don't jump, just take a big step. There's landing on the other aide. You can't see it from there," he gestured with his chin to the girls. "It is bigger than it looks. It's slippery. So grab the rock. Keep your balance." He crouched slightly.

"Don't jump. The landing is lower. Let gravity take you to the other side," Greg said.

"If you jump you may slip," Don said.

"What if you slip?" Terasa asked.

"No one has slipped yet," Don said.

"The undertow in that crack would suck" Harry said. Greg reacted with a smile. Terasa leaned against the cliff face.

The air around them rushed down into the void. There was a backbeat of motion below, an echo of the general movement of water in the basin.

Don twisted his body so those who wanted to examine the fissure could make a view.

They all listened to the waves. Don turned to the gap; shifted his weight, and stretched out his right leg letting his body follow through - - -> landing on the rock face below. Fiona thought he did it between sound + vision - the beat between the bass of the ocean and the high hat of the wind. The water retreated from the crack creating a down draft. They all lowered their stances instinctively.

"You made it look so easy," Terasa said, stepping down the rock ledge to where Don just stood. Don turned to face the rock and took a short sidestep on the wide ledge. Over his shoulder he said to Terasa, "I can count you down."

He reached out.

Teresa moved down. The others shifted behind her. She turned back to the group, her body in retreat. Her foot slipped. Both legs swept out. She went into free fall. Her head dropped, mouth open. Her face slammed onto the rock where her feet had been. Her body pivoted, like a falling fork. Her arms loosely waved. The back of her head hammered on rock below Don's feet. She dissolved down the crack.

Light eclipsed. Movement ceased. Space collapsed. The sky fell. Oceans morphed into clouds of hydrogen and oxygen. Rock vaporized. Protons decayed. Elemental dust imploded. Quark spirals corkscrewed to the center of the collapsing earth. No light. No energy.

Fiona watched the world stop and collapse into something she could put in the palm of her hand. Teresa's scream had finished. Waves curled on the horizon. Fiona looked up.

Radiogram from material found at Beothuk summer camp, Avalon coast

Time Itself

The speed of light squared is time itself. Time only exists if things are moving. Things can only be said to be moving if there is an observer. The observer brings light.

The math shows planets collapsing. Some force, or lack of force, will reduce everything in the planet to elemental pieces, all of which will be compressed into a shape no bigger than a sugar cube. That's what the math shows. That's what we think we see in the stars. We launch telescopes, take pictures, and they show the math to be true.

All we have done is ask the math to help us. It does an amazing job of keeping track. And all math is is relationships. There is always an equals sign. We see something and try to figure it out. The math suggests two different things can be the same. We agree they are.

And math is understood by everyone, no matter their spoken language. It is how the world speaks to us.

Fiona was presented with a 'minus one' real life situation. The math was broken. Minus one equalled zero. It made no sense, this extinguished spark of innocence.

Antitocia

[Events before the Event, where characters gather.]

☺loveguns

Arrivals, St. John's Airport Security Camera

THE SIGN MARKING the carousel was probably busted. The characters in the display could have been Klingon, but for all Leonard knew they may as well have been Tagalog. The airport had become truly international and it was anyone's guess what planes from what countries were parked at the terminal. Direct fights to Abu Dhabi, Moscow, China (over the pole), and Rio de Janeiro were all being tried out. The Lufthansa arrival from Berlin was a well-established route, ever since the Germans started building the 'plug' in the Southside Hills, called the Atlas Center.

The Southside Hills are solid bedrock, a piece of the box spring mattress of the crust's geology folded up and tilted vertically, it's edge sticking up forming the ocean side of the city's harbour. Seismic measurements indicated this massive slab of rock to be one of the most stable places on the planet. A consortium of German firms concluded inside the rock would make a great place to make seismic instruments, precision optics, and nanopharmaceuticals, amongst other things.

First they erected two massive vertical wind turbines. These provided power for hundreds of laser beams used for cutting a gigantic tapered plug out of the mountain. The depth of the plug was 500 feet, its diameter slightly more than 200 feet. The plan was once the vertical cuts had been made devices would be lowered to make the dissecting cut across the bottom of this granite plug. Sonar, laser and streams of water were to be used. Once cleared, the whole plug would be raised hydraulically by pumping oil under the base. Massive shims would be inserted along the sides, giving enough clearance for crews to descend for the work of carving out a series of 2500 foot square rooms vertically spaced 50 feet apart. Three elevator shafts, and some claustrophobic staircases, would be the permanent access points once the shims were relaxed and the plug lowered back onto the rock.

Leonard was amazed they had made the circular vertical cut in less than six months, and he felt terrible for the Germans who were ashamed the circle was off by two millimeters from being perfectly round.

"Shit, I have trouble most days getting the buttons on my shirt lined up," he had said to Bud. "World organizations celebrate 'Gros Mourne', our Massive Tragedy."

Leonard's cell phone rang. It was Colleen.

"Mr Burnett called. He is stuck in Deer Lake. He must have taken the wrong flight," she said. "He has to wait for a rental before he gets in."

Leonard had wondered what happened to the journalist.

"I am waiting for this crowd to disembark. No sign." Leonard scanned the passengers.

"Danke-jen. The place is spotless."

"Don't..." the call was disconnected.

The characters on the Arrival display flashed legible characters "LTH 0802" which must have been the flight they were arriving on. The characters exploded into random red patterns, flickered "☺ loveguns" twice and went back to being all fucked up.

"That's the text I just sent my boyfriend. My god!" a young woman next to him said out loud. Leonard instinctively moved away from her, like a death beam was lining her up and he wanted to avoid the crispy smell.

The door to the international customs opened and passengers trickled out. Leonard held up a sign lettered 'Antitocia'.

Most of the arrivals trudged through the door with their heads down, referencing hand held devices, deadheading to cars and taxis. After a minute a group, which must have been his guests, sifted through the doors. Most of them had their noses in the air, sniffing the salt, their eyes ready to read the sky, encumbered by a noise deadening ceiling.

There was one lad in the middle of the group with his head down. He was tapping on a phone.

A midsized dark-haired man with one of those beards that looks like a handle approached Leonard.

"Mr Livingstone. I am Ludwig Enjurg." He waited for Leonard to acknowledge himself.

"Welcome to Newfoundland, Ludwig. Hope your flight was good. My van is in the parking lot. We will be at Antitocia in mere minutes."

The lad who was tapping on his phone looked at Leonard and prepared his face to speak English. "How far are we from Father Duffy's Well, Mr Livingstone?"

"Leonard, please. About an hour away, 90 kilometers or so."

Everyone in the group gave a little fist pump.

This crowd wanted to taste the local waters. They seemed like a real group of enthusiasts, from the correspondences Leonard had with enjurg_L043@de.h20.

"We are so excited to be here Leonard. This has been a goal for all of us for many ten years."

The lad got back to tapping on his phone.

"Shall we," said Leonard, indicating the parking lot.

The group did not move. Ludwig excitedly raised his hand, and said "Daxen has a question, Mr Livingstone, he is most... he wants to ask."

The guy who asked about the well said, "I am curious. Why did the people on the famous movie about the American fishermen..." his arm indicated a steep incline... "why did the fisherman simply not go to safety here instead of.." his hand had flattened and took a quick right motion, then it returned to the initial position and he stretched it out..."going all the way to Mass-it-two-chits?"

The group was glad the question had been posed to someone who may have an answer.

"Not sure. Guess they would rather risk dying a terrible death than pay for a gallon of gas here."

The group looked concerned, and confused, like a townie trying to use a chainsaw.

"Economics," Leonard said.

The release was immediate, audible. Many nodding of heads.

Everyone understands the odd things people will do for money, even die, settling accounts.

Southside Hills, Daxen Friedlander's Camera

This is the place

LEONARD TURNED the van into the lane. Past the bush and over a wrinkle of land, they would face his house and business square on. He kissed his fingers and tapped the dash, whispering "This is the place."

When he first came round this turn, with Diane, when they saw the house for the first time, they said, "This is the place" excitedly, in unison. They knew they had found the place where they could live and hopefully prosper for the rest of their lives. That was six or seven years ago now, on the horizon of personal memory.

They had no idea what they were going to do with it, a sprawling 7-bedroom ranch with a wraparound patio, two out buildings and enough parking for six or seven vehicles.

Diane immediately became involved with a group trying to put together a farmer's market in the area. It was thought they could make it a destination for the Stavanger crowd. The problem was there were only a handful of suppliers, and those suppliers couldn't necessarily represent themselves, as they had commitments to other markets. It was the usual collection of local producers of honeys, jams, scented soaps and candles, natural body lotions, sea salts, specialized produce, wooden toys and knitted items.

Diane invited the Farmer's Market Committee to meet at their place to discuss strategies for getting the market in place. By the end of their first meeting they had the whole thing planned, with a three month lead time. The main catch was Diane volunteered to collect all the supplies from all the vendors who couldn't represent themselves. This meant she volunteered Leonard for the traipsing around the Avalon Peninsula dropping in on 20 or so chatty farmers and crafts folk, possibly having somewhat clumsy discussions around money, or cash flow.

He didn't mind at all. Several times they drove around together, filling up the large van with bottles of jams, boxes of scarfs and mitts, baskets of lotions and creams, bales of kale and radishes, and bags of elephant garlic.

The market was set like a store, so the vendors did not need to attend. There was hesitation around some of the setup. Some products would get better display than others. All they knew was whatever they had - sold - and that was what counted most.

Diane put together packages of items, which made it easier for folks who couldn't make a decision. They sold mixed vegetables in small paper bags. Jams were bundled with soaps and honeys in crafty wooden boxes Leonard sourced from Green Bay. Any knitted items were packaged in feathery tissue paper tucked in silky maroon boxes, like a gift from Birks.

It was all branded *Logy Fresh Market.*

It was very popular with the yoga pant crowd.

Diane and Leonard built a breezeway between the house and the two outbuildings. They converted one outbuilding into a studio, resurfaced with hardwood and featuring two large windows from a church the town was dismantling. They rented out the space to a yoga class. The second outbuilding they furbished with the supplies they needed to package the goods for the market. The delivery service for the 'Logy Fresh' brand was picking up.

In six months it was a runaway success. In the seventh month Diane became sick.

Reconstructed via DNA from medical waste – Hebron Lab 17

THERE ARE FEW TIMES in one's life where everything seems to be unfolding as it should. There are few times when everything seems to be lined up, ready to go. Talking here about a big scale kind of alignment, the first view of Eden type thing. There are times when everything seems to fit in your suitcase, and you are an extra hour ahead of schedule at the airport. That's being prepared to get on the plane. We're talking about the times when the plane comes to you, and it seems like it knows where you want to go.

And you tend to remember where you were at those times. So the place where the magic happens carries with it a sense of being special as well.

The turn in the lane, where Leonard and Diane first saw the house, was Leonard's special place.

At this point where the house came into view, Leonard would snap into a full 360 degree annotated view of his neighbours and their narratives. Every time he went around the bend the same thing tended to happen. Though he was looking east at the house, his vision went totally full round, and in saturated tones.

To his right, further down the hill tucked up away from the road was his closest neighbour, Ed Kelly.

Edward Kelly was known as the Nelson Mandela of Newfoundland Independence. He would go around saying that he held no grudge against the Canadians that stole his sovereignty, or to the Brits who traded it away to make money on the Labrador. He would say the Americans who profited from scraping the iron ore off the ground in Labrador to make DeSotos and submarines were not to blame for taking advantage of the sweet deals offered by the Canadians and Brits. He would say 70 years of being treated like a forgotten relative served Newfoundland well in the grand scheme of things. The common interpretation of this stance was something along the lines of "We are so far behind that we are now ahead." That's not what he meant. But he didn't do much to change this populist take on things. The saying was a part of the Newfoundland catechism anyway, and to have his name associated with it elevated him somehow. It was all mindshare.

It was all about willpower. Edward Kelly would say the experience had hardened the will of the people of Newfoundland and Labrador, not weakened it. He would say the desert has been crossed, the sea has been sailed, oil has been discovered and the land of milk and honey was "ours for the taking."

Running as a candidate for the "No to All the Above Party " in the last election he managed to come in second. His campaign had only one promise. If he won he would immediately resign and let the election be called again, until the people thought they had a representative who would stand for all the people in his riding. Pundits said it was a clever tactic to help buy time for the Newfoundland Republican Party, so they could get a better chance at a seat in the provincial legislature. Many said he was simply nuts. The majority actually.

Further off to his right, up the road where it hugged the top of the cliff, was the place where Leonard had seen a '72 Rambler drive around a guardrail and crash into the gully, many years ago. He was 16, on a ride on his motorcycle with his friend Bud, the guy Leonard's son gets his nickname from. They used to like to take their bikes and tear around the twisty roads out here. They had slowed down to take in some of the view when a car coming in the other direction went off the road, drove around a guardrail and then drove off the cliff. They went to the house with a giant rock inside and had the owner call the police and ambulances and they

94

waited all day for them to retrieve the driver. It was a young woman. Bud recognized her, his kindergarten teacher, not much more than 30 years old.

Bud was shaken up - he said he had a dream about her two days previously. The fact was, at 16, the complete chorus of people that Bud could draw on for his dreams was rather limited.

The house with the big rock inside it was the Haley house. The daughter, Michelle, was still living there. She helps Leonard now, taking care of the place when there were guests. She was, and still is, simply lovely. She is one of those people you just want to be around. But she flitters about, always on the go.

A day trader from Wyoming bought the Riche farm, complete with horses, in the pasture just over the hill. Horses, magical creatures, an "offering from Nature to help" as Diane used to say.

Below were two lanes. One, MacCharles Lane, had three houses on small acreages - a cop who covered business fraud, a retired RCMP from Nova Scotia and a guy that has something to do with the Canadian Forces. Leonard suspects he is a spy, and the place is a safehouse. He avoids that lane.

The next treed cul-de-sac, Last Chance Rd, had four houses. Six humanities profs were among them. There were three people in the Symphony, two in the Downtown choir, and two were on the board for the botanical garden, one of whom had made a fortune on a book about how insects eat decomposing bodies in different parts of the world. Leonard figured the propane industry, suppliers to crematoriums, were behind the widespread publicity the coffee table version received in American media. It became the gift of choice several Thanksgivings ago. Leonard stays clear here as well, though they did buy a lot from the market when it first started, African goods he managed to source from Bay D'Espoir.

This was the yoga pant crowd. There was only a dozen or so folks living in the four houses, but they were well involved. They liked long black peppers grown in bogwater and guilt-free coffee.

Directly behind him was the valley of the cove, where the rivulets of the surrounding hills snaked into the ocean. In winter the sounds of snowmobiles drummed towards his place. In summer it was chainsaws and dirtbikes. Three sets of lesbians, two male couplings, a polyamorous circus technician, one guy from Welland who owned the golf shop over on the shopping mecca, his portly wife and their six kids - large family nowadays - lived along the main road, where the valley flattened out to form a small plateau. The old Mechka place was now rented out to a ska band and the O'Reilly farm was in disarray because the youngest, Mackenzie, refused to sign the papers unless someone else paid the taxes, which Marilyn, the oldest, refused to do, unless Mac gave her their Dad's walking stick, which he didn't need because he was in a goddamn wheelchair - all according to Michelle.

At the spot where the streams became a bit of a river stood Beth's house, the first farmhouse in the community, a farmhouse being too far from shore to haul a boat. Beth lived there with her mother, Mayme, who cooked for John Cabot they say. She'll never die, says Michelle.

This is the place where Leonard draws his power, against all odds. He doubts he'll find another. This may be his last charge.

From a lost phone on the barrens, Avalon Wilderness

"IF THEY LOOKED AT YOUR DNA they'd find a Leonard Cohen lyric. Why do you have to save everything? Love everything. Judge everything. Let this one pass."

"I don't judge anything."

"Every witness is a judge. By experiencing these people you are judging them."

Michelle's back tightened like a bow. "They need me Len."

"I need you."

"You have enough of me. This is bad juju. These people are losing it. And they are amongst us."

"The world one hundred feet past my property is bad juju. There's a row of temples a few miles from here where seemingly normal people buy bad juju armaments for their patio."

Leonard stuck his thumbs in his belt. "Who can you get to cover for you?"

"Cover for me! I am not responsible to get people to cover for me."

Michelle stepped towards him, pushing her scent. "Some of these people think you are an alien. They think you have secrets. They say you are sharing these secrets with me. Here. In your wacky house - they call it a temple, a place of power. They think you see the dead."

"Worse has been said about me. I have ten German wack jobs coming in next week for a week. Ten. For a week. I need you for five days. Not two days, skip-a-day, two days".

"I have to tell them you are just an arsehole. An arsehole who thinks he is stuck with this ideal lifestyle, hosting all kinds of people who want to have a chance to experiment with their life. And you don't even get that."

"I get it. I can't feed and do the laundry for ten krauts on the third day. I collapse on the third day. I plan to crash. I need it."

"Len, you don't understand. These people have rituals. Buy more sheets, cheapskate."

"That's exactly why I don't want you to go. Take a raincheck. Do a few Stations of the Cross. Say a Hail Mary."

Mocking: "Protect me. Make the beds."

"Remember your duck dungarees?"

"My workpants."

"Yes" - Michelle started to stand on her toes – "Your workpants. Stolen right off the washline."

"I told you, they were probably taken by one of the crowd from the Trail. Those mainlanders are always jumping in the cove naked. Someone needed some clothes."

"Beth took them. They cut it up in pieces" - she raised both hands to the sides of her head – "and then they passed out the pieces to everyone in the group. The crotch of your 'workpants' are stuffed in the crack of the rocks of Manchu Pichu. The lesbians poked your crotch in a crack in a rock. Get it!"

"The Aztecs were better builders than that."

Michelle's hands rested on Leonard's chest, high, near his neck – "You're next. I am trying to save you. All the parts" - she tapped him on the nose, and stepped back. Turning she pitched – "Phone Beth, See if she can come in for one day."

She stopped in the frame of the doorway – "Bet Beth is busy. Twelve Germans are coming for two weeks, not one."

Like that she was gone, the music of her life stepping down stairs.

"Shit" Leonard said. "We're all retards."

Livingstone Homestead, along trail

A great general wins a battle. A young girl has a solution. A women feeds her child who cannot leave the bed. A man breaks a record. A group has their protests heard. A poet is remembered.

A boy cries wolf. A young criminal is gunned down. A housewife swindles millions. Politicians make a sinister agreement.

A scientist makes a discovery. A comedian gets the last laugh. A woman floats in space. A young couple gets married.

The boy gets the girl. The girl overcomes the odds. The old man passes on wisdom. The woman dies, saving thousands.

A son kills his mother. Two brothers fight for their father's approval. A man covets his brother's wife, and the throne.

A princess becomes a queen. A knight overcomes a deformity.

The painter pledges love to the blind partner. A soldier builds a greenhouse. The spy is found dead, under mysterious circumstances.

A mother carries her dead child down a dirt road. A child cares for her grandmother. A child gets a wish. A young rebel chews on a leaf.

A woman plants a seed. A man says 'Hi'.

Rain falls on a stone, tears roll down a face. A comet flies through space, unnoticed.

Element 26

[Random signal, Bears investigation.]

A scientist zooms in on the sample, returned from a spaceship now lost to the sun. There is movement: hexagon platelets join together to create a capsule. On the surface of a platelet crystals move across magnetic fields. The platelet divides and unfolds, creating another capsule. Material moves on the joins of the new unions. The growth continues, until the capsules suddenly collapse into one another, the seams twisting with the strain. At the center of the new shifting shape two atoms of iron illuminate, one broadcasting red light, the other absorbing all other colours. The construct waits for further instructions.

Type: Notice

From: NF7717044

Subject: Hardware recovered

Deep sea dive HIB-775Ah successful. Incoming data. Will be released after analysis

Current Correspondence

Mysteries have stronger roots than truths

[A moment, defined.]

S HE STEPPED IN FRONT OF HIM and went through the door first, breaking her stride so he would be close behind. Ten feet in, in a corridor of people at the inside entrance of the bar, she stopped, said hi to a friend; someone Leonard barely knew. Diane smiled at him and skootched forward so he could pass.

"Hi" he said.

Leonard pivoted past, his hands perched on her shoulders, face in her hair, and went towards the bar.

There were a surprising number of people he knew little about.

He ordered a stout and checked the immediate space. Erin sat two stools down. He had resolved himself to simply have a lifelong crush on her. And Diane. Being in their space made him feel blessed. Mysteries have stronger roots than truths.

As the first pour finished he turned to check the room. Diane stepped into him, wrapping her arms around him under his jacket, giving him a hug, her fingers on his spine.

Leonard slowly coiled his arms around her. He breathed in the scent of Diane's hair as he scanned the room. Many eyes were on them. He exhaled, drawing her closer.

She sunk her head into his chest, traced her nose on his breastplate, drawing in the air between them.

"So good to see you, Len" - she tilted back, levering her hips against his hands, moving them down – "You are looking good."

"Nice to see you." People were staring. Leonard could make out the groups: associations of people bonded by circumstance, by industry, by neighbourhood.

"How have you been?"

She kissed him on the cheek. He could hear Erin stop midsentence, like a rear speaker cutting out.

"It's not where I've been, it's where I want to be." Her right hand on his hip pushed him away from the bar; her weight shifting.

Diane looked up into his eyes. She lowered her gaze, examined his mouth.

"I don't want to be here. Let's get dessert."

"Dessert."

"Dessert. Share a piece of cheesecake with me."

"Done." Leonard turned, paid for his beer, slid it into the forearm of a long ago geology classmate leaning against the bar. "Cheers mate. Your paper is slate." The chap nodded, recognizing the phrase of their former teacher.

Diane turned and they walked the gauntlet of wry smiles back through the bar. And that was it. They started their life together, thirty years after they first met.

BUD WAS THERE TO HELP unload the van. Colleen met the visitors in the open foyer. Leonard gave them a quick walk along the veranda of the house, pointing out the cove, the tract of the river in the valley, and the path of the trail. He indicated a place well up the large rocky hill where there was a spring known only to the locals.

"WiFi. Do you facilitate wi-fi?" the guy with the invisible frame glasses asked Leonard.

"We do. But we keep it off for the guests."

The man walked across the veranda, made his way through the others going into the house, and then started chatting with two of the arriving guests.

Leonard noticed all the visitors were wearing shades of green and grey. One had a green scarf with red trim. Leonard never understood scarfs as a clothing accessory. What were they for? Outbreaks of nearby anarchy? Casual looting? Ninja rope tricks?

Leonard looked down to the road. There was a large, new Cadillac crawling along, just past the laneway to his property.

A smallish man, the one with the scarf, sporting hairy Neil Young sideburns, thumbed away on his phone. Two others, a gal with a ponytail and a slight man Leonard figured must have been a born premature, seemed to adjust their orientation towards the texter. They slowly raised palms parallel to the ground. Having seemingly finished, the texter spoke in a low deliberate voice.

"Water, from the wild, tames us," he pronounced in clear English.

Leonard couldn't see the two with their backs to him, but he clearly saw the texter tilt his head back and stick out his tongue, catching imaginary rain.

Leonard walked into the house, giving a nod to Colleen as he passed into the large feature room. Michelle had laid out a small buffet, and was adjusting a steamer. A couple of the guests had started piling food on plates. The others chained in behind.

Leonard was pleased. Colleen was a great help, and Michelle had made the place seem warm and comforting. It smelled great; fresh squeezed cranberry juice and blueberry vinaigrette filled the air.

"Here you go, luv," Michelle said handing out glasses of water poured from the tap. Locally bottled water, in glass milkbottles, sat untouched.

"Have a bite to eat. Then we'll show you your rooms," he announced. "We'll go for a quick walk along the trail, have a quick boil up at Spring Lookout, and have an early night. I figure you must be hungry, need a stretch, a nap, before tomorrow."

"Your water," the bookish type started, the others pausing. "Your wild water, your well water, is excellent." The others nodded.

Leonard wondered if there was any way he could slip in a shot of absinthe before they left on the walk. At least one.

He had started the day at 7am by smoking a large doobie on the deck. Bud's weed with some black hash an adventure tourist had given him. The dude came over on a Portuguese cargo ship, Lisbon to St. John's. It was loading up on Newfoundland cod and he had a lot of this great black hash, the currency of sailors.

On the deck, in between draws, he said out loud to the trees descending to the shore, "Why do you smoke weed all by yourself on your deck?" The wind was indifferent. "It's because I can!" he answered.

He wanted to have a good buzz for when Michelle arrived at 7:30am. He wanted to drink her in.

Michelle was always on time. Always. Some folks pitied her, as they felt she lacked options. She never travelled far from the bay. The quick conjecture was she could barely cobble together a life.

But she was the opposite. Her life fit her. It worked. She followed the wind given her. She had a great sense of the common denominators of the human experience. Her age put all this in perspective.

Perspective is the most important part of life. It means you are looking. You have imagined a space ahead. You are going somewhere.

Michelle saw a lot of people without perspective. They had a storm of energies around them, unfocused. Some were damaged, crippled by some early strangeness, like some mutated 'life gene'. Family was always in there. Being aware of the fault can fix it, but self-reflective thought experiments rarely include experiences you have not had, but need.

To fix yourself, to know what you lack, to address your weaknesses, is rare.

And that is exactly what made Michelle tick. She did what she needed to do, rather than doing what she wanted to do. What people really want, is to do what they need to do.

For now, it seemed Michelle needed to help Leonard. He is a wonderful man. He has had a wonderful life. He absorbed Diane's loss. He survived it. The second disaster, after Bud's mom, many years ago. The world, or what was left of it, was in front of them.

She liked who he was, how he kept going, how he built this oddball business. She was helping Leonard fit into his life.

Livingstone Homestead, along trail, compost

Bud approached Leonard with the phone in his hand.

"Dad, there are 6 messages on the phone."

"I don't like answering the phone."

"Have you listened to the messages?"

"I need someone to do that for me."

"Hard to run a business if you don't answer the phone."

"Let them book online. Pay online."

"Did you forget the code?"

"If it's not a local call, I don't answer. Could be Batswabi someplace and cost me my house and home, just answering the phone."

"Dad..." Bud called in for messages.

Leonard turned towards the room. The Germans had settled in nicely. He could tell they felt comfortable. The food smelled great. Michelle had outdone herself.

She said to him the Germans were all about the water. They wanted their food cooked in local water, their beer and other beverages to be made with local water. They wanted fruits and berries sourced locally so they could be sure they all had local water.

They also wanted a sauna, so they could sweat a lot. Leonard had managed to locate a few old units that used to be on the American Base. The one person saunas where the head stuck out of the top and looked like they had been eaten by a washing machine. The saunas were made out of battleship steel, from the time when a great many battleships were made. The steel was smelted from Labrador ore.

Michelle had served up blueberries, candied dandelion, caramelized cod tongues, moose stew, cod roe in partridgeberry sauce served on shortbread sitting on ice chips from a glacier, and seaweed soaked in cinnamon wrapped around slices of apple, served on warmed flatstones in pools of honey.

One of the Germans, sporting a turtleneck, was picking samples from each tray and placing them in small glass jars.

"Midnight snacks?" Leonard asked.

"For analysis. I will weigh and photograph. Then we will dehydrate, and determine the water content."

"You guys are quite serious," Leonard said.

"We are here for transformation. Our experience and knowledge base tells us it may take up to six days for us to purge ourselves of the foreign matter and be totally re-aquifed. The body is 60% water, and now we are 60% German water, except Drewgen who was in Amsterdam, so he is 20% beer." He laughed. "We want to be 60% Avalon water. It will take six days, perhaps."

"I don't have many towels, so if you can go easy on the saunas. I'll show them to you when we get settled."

"Day next perhaps. We will start with enemas this evening and tomorrow morning."

Leonard wanted to think he heard 'enemies' not 'enemas'. He was far more comfortable with the idea of guests toting around lugers than guests with tubes stuck in the arses, siphoning shitjuce. People will try anything, especially if it's at someone else's place.

"We will do some bioelectrical impedance analysis this evening. We do mass spectrometry in the lab. Between us, we will consume about 400 litres of your water over the next ten days."

Leonard hasn't seen a crowd this nuts since the 'breathing Buddhists' last summer. They never said a word all week. They breathed in the problems of the world and exhaled love and joy, apparently.

Leonard caught one of them drinking his own pee. Pissed in a beer glass and gulped it down.

Leonard had to air the place out when they left. Peace can have a foul smell, if concentrated.

"We are here for many things, many experiences, but Father Duffy's Well will be the top of our peak here."

Leonard reached over and grabbed the stickers and a marker. "For name tags. You are..?"

"Albert, Mr Livingstone."

One of the others joined them. A Kristophe. "These apples are to kill for."

"We have a cider. We will save that for later. Aqua vitae."

Bud approached. Leonard stepped aside so they could speak in private.

"You have 6 messages from this guy in Zurich, Dad. It's about the prize. No wonder you never heard about it."

"Right. That English lad should be here soon," Leonard said. "Have you had a chance to look at the saunas yet?"

"Yes. It should work fine."

"No smell?"

"Fir needles and pine tar. These guys will be very relaxed."

Bud had made pellets for the sauna in ice trays consisting of fir needles, pine tar, sawdust, molasses and Newfie Kush marijuana. The smouldering pellets heated iron plates in the units, and dripping water created the soothing steam. Leonard's plan was to have these guys slightly buzzed with whatever means possible for the next two weeks. These guys were in for a bake.

"Thanks son. We're gonna need to soothe this crowd down. Intense crew."

"I tried it on Ed Kelly last night. Michelle said there hasn't been a sign of him," Bud said.

"Excellent." It would keep Ed out of his hair for a few days, but he might come back for more.

"Stay away from the apples. I soaked the seaweed in mushroom tea. The cinnamon hides the taste, or I should say the mushroom tea sharpens the cinnamon. Two slices and you are Side B. Three, you'll be lucky to have a dial tone."

"I have a gig for Colleen, Dad. She is going to help with the Downtown Creative Collective. She's not gonna be able to help around here for much longer."

Leonard stared at his son. He was deciding if he should hate his only child.

"We'll find someone else, Dad. Someone we can trust. Honest."

"Everyone gets away with what they can get away with. I think Colleen is stealing my pants."

Bud scratched his head. His dad was drifting off.

"Michelle says it's the lesbians." Leonard popped a slice of apple in his mouth and sucked the juices. "I wanna believe it's someone, anyone, else." His face orchestrated a series of grimaces.

"Excuse me, Albert. I have to ask that you not take a sample of the apples. It's a recipe from my dear late partner, and it is a bit of a specialty item for us. We do not allow specimens of this particular item to be taken off the property."

"Property" Kristophe said. "Bad machine."

"Certainly, Mr Livingstone. We have plenty of apple data. No problem." He handed Leonard the jar. Leonard removed the slice, popped it in his mouth, and held up the empty jar. "I will rinse this out."

He turned and went to the sink. He looked out the window at Ed Kelly's. No sign. Then he forgot where he was. Forgot his name. He forgot who he was. All he could see was the treed valley. All he could hear was the ocean. All he could smell was the colour blue. He was Side B.

"1963!" he shouted to himself in his own mind. "That's the code for the telephone messages." He hadn't remembered the code for over a year.

Recreational filter, several subjects

Intermission

[These findings were similar in all subjects. One extract is
directly from Leonard Livingstone, but traces of his view are
shared. Leonard had the strongest signal.]

Capistrum navitas

Sure, hands are important. Right brain, left brain, proteins, diets, medicine, writing, scientific method, singularity of deities, happy hour, roller coasters and rock-n-roll have all been significant forces in the development of humankind into what we are today. Evolution, Communism, Revolution, free trade and Republicanism all play a part. But what makes humans modern, what separates us from 99% of previous human experience, is the harnessing of energy.

Once we started to move electrons around, human life entered a whole new era.

Able to see what couldn't be seen, with light when it used to be dark. Able to heat where it couldn't be heated. Able to move what couldn't be moved. Able to hear what couldn't be heard.

The harvesting of energy has made all the difference.

We have Hollywood, Jaguars, fresh avocados, telephones and pictures of outer space because we started playing with fire we can't see, to move fire along wires and through the air itself.

The shadow on the wall is from our own source of light. Make a rabbit, or a dog, in the night.

For some reason Leonard was led to believe that his lineage as a human, one that organized itself to eventually lead to his present form of government, involved the fucking Etruscans. The Jewish thing was like an opening act for the seeding of Rome. Then the Catholics. Then the Fights. Then the fights amongst ourselves. And now there was a precarious time of global peace, while we wait for the giant in South Asia to do whatever it will do.

It looks like Leonard's crowd is losing the battle. They have to believe in the long term.

Leonard's ancestors used to say they believed in the long term, to their death. Their very own existence depended on people, who they were somehow connected with, to be in power. To have someone in authority from a different place, speaking a different language, often meant you were a slave. You would be last on the list to receive any of the bounty from the earth. So you might as well die fighting for what you know, because there is no second place in a war. Winners and losers. Winners control the larder.

The types of governing systems of societies had been relatively few, mainly different lineages of kings and queens, with their appropriate war lords and eunuchs.

The museums Leonard's forebears left for him were full of English, European, Mediterranean, and Middle Eastern artifacts: statues, columns, pottery and jewelry. The gift of self-expression, or art for the celebration of the individual, has only been around since the announcement of North America. There was a renaissance caused by the creation of a middle class, which itself was an outcome of a great plague.

The people who did live here, the natives who walked and sailed over from the Asias tens of thousands of years ago, are having a tough time fighting for storage and display space in the museums. They are essentially forgotten.

And the Asians are coming again, this time by plane.

Leonard believes his generations beyond will see the last two hundred years as one of massive change, of the pursuit of discovery, and the settlement of differences. The results of shared discovery showing us we have few options, as we have limited quarrels - they can be worked out - but we all share the same sky and drink the same water. We use the energy of the world, and the world carries on.

There are other lineages, other histories of warriors and aristocrats, philosophers and courtesans. There is no way to know them all. The stories you are told at a young age form the root of your understanding. Other stories, from other people, are measured against this understanding, and always fall short.

The people on the bleeding edge of our civilization, people in the west, people in western North America, are the people most likely to abandon their core beliefs and reinvent themselves. Far away from the yoke of history, they are the people who create our collective 'now'. They, the 'StarChilds' and the 'Fubar901s', do not even know what a fucking Etruscan looks like, unless they are characters in movies.

On the east coast the Etruscans still own the shops, and monitor the burying of the dead.

It's funny and sad that often large-scale human conflicts have different religious beliefs as the main points of contention. It's distressing because in all cases the religious argument is based on a narrative that can't be seen: different views of the afterlife.

No one has ever reported from the afterlife. It's like a fundamental law of human existence for fuck's sake. You live. You die. That's all we know. You are experiencing **Step One:** *Living*, and you are guaranteed to experience **Step Two:** *Dead*. The sun rises and sets.

If anyone has been dead and come back, where are the pictures? They haven't even come back with a souvenir crushed copper penny. It hasn't happened. Ever. That is what makes it funny, cause you just have to laugh at the notion that doing something while you are alive has any effect on your existence, if there is any, when you are dead.

You go back to the earth. Back to water and food for other life. No one can say they represent conquering this truth. If they do, they are lying.

People who say they know what happens to dead people are merely sharing a wish, a fantasy. They have a story draped over the arc of life, explaining existence in simple terms. To say we do not know is the clearest of statements. But people cannot claim authority if they do not put forth an explanation to the basic question all people have.

Getting these people confused with folks who can act for the much greater good is easy with a bit of magic, a few relics, and some compelling stories reminding us we are descended from heroes. We accept our heroes at their word. Our heroes built a mean fucking column and wore a lot of gold.

We have developed a new definition of coward. We know the gods are mere men, tied to stones, and yet we do not put up a fight. We feed them when we should be starving them. Mysteries have stronger roots than truth.

Found on Beth's camera

Alone

Extraction

`[ Backstory, extracted from light signatures captured in jewels, and trace nuclear narratives. ]`

Furlongs of Fortune

"**T**HEY CALL THEM 'Extractive Industries.' That should provide a clue. Fishery, mines, lumber, anything that can be loaded on a ship and sent away. That's all they're interested in."

Only three days into the voyage and this chap has Dennis Livingstone pegged as a socialist.

"Be careful what you say mate," Dennis gestured towards the First Class section.

"Merely conversation. Not looking for trouble." The man swooped his hands palms open to his side, as if showing he was unarmed. The thrust of his chest suggested to Dennis any 'conversation' with this man could quickly boil to a tempest, a kind of test. This would serve as an entry into a chapter of mischief. Dennis was used to this quick bravado, he relished it, but he had good reason to stay below the line. At least for a few more weeks.

The RMS Newfoundland was much more powerful than the converted tea junker SS Brunswick. It had a

lot further to sail - Liverpool to St. John's compared to Chichester to Liverpool – Dennis' first leg on this sudden journey.

Hard to lay low when the other 90 common passengers all seem to want to get to know you.

A May sailing. The year's first. The year being 1933. Reports of the riots shutting down the government in the Dominion of Newfoundland the previous month were all the talk. First class had extra security.

The passage to Liverpool from Chichester, his home town, had almost killed him, twice. That's not exactly precise. Getting to Liverpool had been difficult. He was almost robbed in Bristol en route, while the SS Brunswick berthed to exchange fares. Getting robbed would have been disastrous. He left one lad with a broken foot and another with a messed up neck, he figured. If he had been robbed, or if his assault on his robbers had come under investigation, his world would have turned dark.

The second time he almost died, or was threatened with a loss of freedom, was during next leg of the journey, the sailing from Bristol to Liverpool aboard the SS Brunswick

He decided to dine, and in the crowded room he took a small table in the corner with a view. He was soon joined by a Detective Clive Galvin, of Scotland Yard. The detective commented that while they were berthed in Bristol there had been a vicious attack on two young unfortunates, a deaf mute and a cripple. The deaf mute had been rendered crippled by the attack, and the cripple could no longer speak, due to an injury upon his throat.

Dennis could not suppress a fantastic laugh at the report of the beating he lashed out.

"I fail to see this as a formula for mirth," the detective said.

"You say…" Dennis held onto his ribs where the mute cracked him. "You say the mute…" he had to stop or finish, the officer was looking concerned. "You say the mute is now crippled. The crippled is now mute." He could barely finish.

Dennis managed a smile, and a shrug. The laugh driveling through his face and shoulders.

"My youngest is crippled," Mr Galvin said. "Terrible bit of work for all of us." He looked stern. "I wish the missus was mute in his stead." The officer let out a deep laugh, a laugh he thoroughly enjoyed, sharing his pains with a stranger, sailing from his troubles. Dennis sighed with relief. The officer was forgetting about the beating.

"I am going to Newfoundland," Dennis said. "Are you terminating in Liverpool?"

"Yes. I will be there for five days. Have a new case, a jewel theft of some renown, and there are several people in Liverpool with important background information," the detective shared.

The copper was back on Dennis' station, about to tie up it seemed.

"Liverpool. Never been. The Newfoundland leaves in two days. Perhaps I can get my sea legs before she leaves."

"Ships leave me wobbly," the Mr Galvin said.

"I can't imagine going by aeroplane. Where would they put the dining room?"

"My young Jimmy says when he gets older flights across the Atlantic will be more common than steamships."

"Give me a ship with three engines, rather than an aeroplane with two," Dennis said. "Beg your pardon, I must go and have a short pipe. My stomach is a bit upset."

He pushed himself away from the table and headed for the nearest door to the deck, starboard. His heart was pounding, hands sweating. He wanted to progress across the room with solid footing, to hide the fact he really wanted to jump like a rabbit. Experience told him you do not run away from a copper if you do not want to be chased. He imagined himself as one of the King's horses in a grand parade, but he looked more like a drunk donkey. As long as he did not run, which would be wholly without profit, as there is nowhere to hide on a small ship.

The sea air calmed Dennis down. He leaned against the wall of the main cabins and watched the rain fall over the canopy across the deck back into the sea. It would take a few days to get to his brother Gerry's place in St. John's, Newfoundland. Gerry had done well, working as a printer, married with a young boy of his own. In fact, Dennis may be an uncle to one or two more by now. It would be good to visit his younger brother in the colony, and escape his troubles.

So, the coppers knew about the jewels, about Mellor. His arrival in Chichester must be under their glass. Setting up an antique shop always brings suspicion as well. Dennis put his hand into the Italian leather satchel sashed across his body, searching for the pipe and tobacco. The pouch containing them was untied, unlike the others, which were tightly bound. He reached in and his fingers traced the edge of the pages of a small book. He wanted to look at it again. Not now, wait till the morning. In his cabin.

* * *

A few days previous he saw Frank Shackleton, the disgraced brother of the explorer, take some coin out o this satchel. Dennis figured there must be more coin.

Dennis had brought some ale, cheese, eggs and biscuit from the Resting Owl to Shackleton's new business. Dennis was running errands in return for food from the hawks who owned the Owl. This day, Mr Shackleton and his motley crew could not eat at the pub, as they needed to be present for the delivery of goods from an estate for an auction.

Shackleton was an odd fellow, a real anti-hero. He arrived in Chichester and set up a new business using the name 'Mellor'. His proper name was too well known in England, thanks to his brother's tale in Antarctica and rumours of his own disgraceful involvement with the Royal family.

Dennis saw Shackleton stuff the bag behind a trunk in the office, but Shackleton had not seen him. Shackleton and his friends assumed the tipsy server would be long gone. He wasn't. Dennis was having a pleasurable shit in the loo, with a view to the back portion of the nook to the great room.

Dennis heard all the men laugh and shout crude insults. Howling. He darted into the office and grabbed the bag, exiting through a broken section at the back of the loo, out along the busy pier. He put the bag in a burlap satchel of his own. He walked along to the piers where heavier ships were being loaded, and familiars were fewer. Standing under an archway leading to boarding houses in the inner harbour he checked the contents of Mr. Mellor's leather bag.

A small black notebook. Plenty of money, more than Dennis hoped for. A fine pipe. Three fingers of black hashish. Two vials of coca powder. And six different pieces of heavy jewelry.

The small black book had 'Frank Shackleton' written on the inside front cover, itself tucked under a new sleeve over the covers. The inside front page read *'Property of Frank Mellor - Antiques proprietor, Cheshestire.'* A few pages had been torn from the book before this current front page.

Frank Shackleton. Brother of Ernest, famed explorer. Vagabond who stole the Irish Crown jewels in 1907. Changes his name and sets up an antiques shop in the town Dennis called home – Chichester, 25 years on.

The tap against the stone wall behind the archway four or five feet to Dennis' right, aft, caught him off guard. He dropped the leather bag back into the burlap satchel.

"State your business," came the command. It was a copper. It's been a few days of coppers. This was the first.

"The passenger pier. I am twisted around I fear," Dennis stammered.

"Line?" the officer asked.

"Newfoundland," Dennis said. "Furney?"

"Furness line. Out of Liverpool, RMS Newfoundland," the policeman offered. "Carriage on the Anchor Line."

Dennis stared at the copper dumbly. He was not acting.

"The Newfoundland sails from Liverpool. A part of the Furness line. This is Chichester." The policeman tapped his club on the stone wall to bring attention to the situation. "To get to Liverpool you book passage on the Anchor Line. The Brunswick, SS Brunswick. First to Bristol for half a day. Three piers along. You better hurry, whistles have steamed."

"Thank you sir. I must run. Regards."

Dennis walked to the pier using all the shortcuts he knew. Every new furlong offered fortune.

That is the start of the journey of how the Irish Crown jewels made their way into Leonard's house, beneath some floorboards. Dennis's brother Gerald was Leonard's dad.

The Marquis de Lorne, the Governor and Constable of Windsor Castle was an accomplice of Frank Shackleton in the stealing of Irish Crown jewels. Rumour was they were all part of a group of men who staged a homosexual orgy and stole the jewels during the tryst. A Tryst Heist so to speak. Despite the outrage at the theft of the jewels the affair was not officially investigated, as The Marquis de Lorne – John Campbell, 9th Duke of Argyll - was married to Queen Victoria's daughter, Louise.

The Marquis de Lorne was the 4th Governor General of Canada. He was snubbed by Oscar Wilde when Wilde visited Ottawa in 1882, as part of his tour of the Americas evangelizing aestheticism. Wilde was introducing art to people's lives with the same zeal as the painters who were trying to bring life to art, the Impressionists. In Ottawa, Wilde met Frances Richards, a portrait artist. She would paint a portrait of Wilde in later years, when she resided in Europe. That portrait was the inspiration for Wilde's book "The Picture of Dorian Grey ", published 1890.

None of the characters in this collection have ever read "The Picture of Dorian Grey." There are quite a few who have read "Treasure Island " by Robert Louis Stevenson, published 1883.

Memory of Crowsnest, assembled via radio capture

Retrieved from discarded cathode ray tube.

Mare Liberum

[Very clear signal from a repository of jewels and some pottery shards. A band of matching vibrations were tuned and recorded for this excerpt. This assortment is from the time of the early days of photography - mechanical and chemical visual recording - from the 1820s to the 1840s.]

The Free Sea

THE SOUND OF BELLS over the water indicated John Richards had reached his navigation point. Divine luck guided him here. He was near the island where Ira Bridgewater was landside. The bells were tuned as the strings of a guitar, and when they swayed – they were on ropes suspended between two trees – they played.

For a line on safe passage John Richards had to ring back. Ring the bell wrong, and passage would be ignored. Ring it correctly, there were no guarantees he could ever leave.

Ira Bridgewater was an old friend of John's father, Richard Richards the Third. He was the original member of a group of outlaws living on a small island, off the south coast of Cuba – the Oriente – ten leagues west of Chivirico, at the foot of the Sierra Maestra Mountains. Bridgewater was the first of many sailors who jumped ship and made this paradise their home. RR3 would make trade with Bridgewater, at this secret sanctuary, when the elder Richards ran exchange out of Havana for the British. This was before John's time.

John Richards was in a small Bermuda sloop, the 'Logy Loop'. It lay low in the water, able to cut through like a shark's fin, with ballast of Panamanian potting clay below the boards keeping her belly wet.

Two bags of potting clay were speckled with Peruvian Blue opals and coin blank ingots of Spanish silver.

Released from the British authority, alone sailing from Portobello, Panama, John Richards was following a makeshift plan. The jewels he had, used to belong to treasure hunters. The treasure hunters he just robbed were making their way back to the port of St. John's, John Richards home town.

For now, Richards focus is on getting his opals and silver baked in pottery. Large chafing dishes is the plan. He needs proper passage from Havana to the Avalon, and he doesn't want to risk being found, with pieces of silver, by ruthless men, on the Caribbean Sea, the water where Spanish silver knows no magistrate.

Bridgewater, and his society, could grant him sanctuary, long enough for the potting. Or not.

Ira Bridgewater was the first of the Top Men of the Oriente. During the reign of Mad King George, Richard Richards the Third had dropped Bridgewater off with provisions on the largest island of the tiny archipelago off the south coast of Cuba. RR3 quietly recruited more inhabitants, from the port of Havana, to join Ira. Men and women looking for freedom, away from the British flag, and used to living by the codes of the sea, by agreement amongst equals, were attracted to the independent colony. No one wanted to return to an Ireland under British rule.

There were few laws for the informal colony. First rule was once you arrived, you could never leave. Second rule was for a period up to year after your arrival, all titled members of the society could kill you without reproach. Title was given after a year. Any women who were not liked, were not killed. They were quarantined to their own section of beach, opposite a salt white lagoon, beneath insurmountable cliffs.

These men would not practice slavery, but every one of them knew how to do a good shun.

The shallow rocky waters around the islands made attack difficult. Many pirates may have wanted the men, most would settle for the stored riches. The bells drew them into the shallows, the high waves smashed them along shards of rock.

The Top Men of the Oriente were so well hidden, so protective of their location, they had no songs in their name.

Richard Richards the Third had a song. He sang it to John, on his knee.

> Bells mark the shores,
> Of free sailors and whores,
> Living wild on the ocean blue.
> Dogs get to bark,
> And men fed to sharks,
> On the shore of the White Lagoon.
> Sad sisters shunned,
> And all kings are done,
> On the isles of the White Lagoon.
> All live as one,
> On the Isles of Top Men,
> Beneath the Caribbean moon.
> Never to be found.
> Never to be found, my lad.
> Not lost, yet not found.
> Land; new not found.

John's father had taught John the signal he made with a small bell to mark his arrival off the shallow shores. He tapped it out with his fingers; an old, quick, shanty, familiar to those on the Labrador.

Tip-Tappity tap tap, Tap tap, Tap tap,

Tip-Tappity tap tap, Tap tap, Tip-tap, – Tap Tap

Ira Bridgewater and his men had always granted RR3 safe passage.

John hoped the signal was remembered, thirty years on. He hoped his father was still good in the Men's hearts, and he would be granted short sanctuary, exempt from the society's command.

He had placed his life in the hands of the fates, and they allowed him to reach these shores, with Salty, a black St. John's dog.

———◆———

Back in Panama, John watched the mule trains for the British authorities.

Panama was a newly minted independent state in 1841, and the country was flooded with all manners of people, from various territories and large enterprises, prodding around, trying to build favour. A lot of the activity was around the talk of building a clear passage from the Atlantic to the Pacific, by rail and perhaps by canal. The small country was seen as a keystone of the territory recently called New Granada, now dividing into states such as Columbia, Venezuela, and Peru. The French, Americans, Spanish and British were all looking for favour amongst those who thought they were in charge.

The mule route was the main connection between the oceans, used by sailors and prospectors under many flags and banners. The King's Road, built by the Spanish, who called it the Camino Real trail, was the main thoroughfare. Users of the trail needed horses and mules to transport their cargo, so the British set John Richards up with a livery service, to could keep an eye on the people and goods moving between the oceans.

John operated the service with Rambinder, a strapping Sikh who wore a silk tartan turban. His ancestors had been involved in the secret Scottish silk trade. They smuggled worms and mulberry bushes, from the orient to the highlands, to grow silk in Scotland. Their story is a different thread.

John and Rambinder plied the route between Nombre de Diós and Porto Bella, the last section of the dangerous and challenging overland route between the oceans, the Pacific and the Caribbean.

John recognized the fellow Newfoundlanders as they inquired around the Name of God post for a mule train and horses. One was Captain Keating. The other, a young man, with a distinctive cut of cloth worn by St. John's seamen, pants made from light sail. They were treasure hunters, from St. John's, with knowledge about the Lima treasure.

He expected he wouldn't be their top choice, if they knew he was familiar with Duckworth and Water Streets, so he spoke in sailor's French, as a disguise. He told them he had a train ready to go. They were needed in Porto Bella and had to return immediately anyway. This allowed him to sweeten the price, and capture their business.

Captain Keating and younger Billy Boag loaded his mules with treasure they would later tell everyone they didn't find. The jewels and blank pieces of silver were spread amongst petrified bones, exotic botanical samplings and bundled Aztec serving dishes. In passing, they said they dealt in tropical exotics, and were headed to Bermuda via Havana, or Barbados, depending on the winds.

They acted as top men, burdened by the recent loss of Billy's father, Captain Boag. He drowned whilst they were in Panama town, eaten by sharks. They buried his arm, the only piece recovered, in the port cemetery, a few days earlier.

John Richards had learned of this expedition a year earlier, while back in St. John's.

At the London Tavern, Richards' sister's friend William Bray, told him Keating was looking for backers, or partners, to capture the Spanish silver and gold stolen many years ago by a Captain Marion Thompson, the most wanted man in British and Spanish ports.

Word was Thompson was hiding in Cochrane's cabin, up on the lake that fed Quidi Vidi.

"Leave the Billy " was the saying William Bray told Richards that started the tale.

Richards had mentioned he had been given several large, empty rum barrels – hogsheads - if he could get them out of the storeroom in Kings Cove. He had no way to get them up to Georgetown. He needed a cart with a horse, and inquired with William.

"Leave the Billy," Bray said.

"What does that mean, 'Leave the Billy' – a Galway saying?"

"A Captain Thompson saying. When his crew were hiding the Lima treasure on the island, there was a gold statue, solid gold, which weighed more than five men. The great Virgin Mary got stuck in the sand on the beach and they couldn't move it. So they buried it. Thompson said if they ever managed to get it in the jungle they would have had to 'leave the billy' eventually. It was too stubborn, like a goat. Too great a weight. Leave the hogsheads. Billy the goats."

On the Camino Real, a few miles past the quarry, John, Rambinder and the St. John's men were swarmed by a pack of Scottish halfbreeds. The wild tribe rushed out of the jungle, knocking the travellers to the ground and raiding their bags, disappearing back

134

into the bush. Richards saw a bundle let loose, its counterpart on the other side of the mule having been cut away. He hid the leather pack under the blanket of his horse during the fray. Rambinder chased the naked ginger herd into the jungle.

Keating laughed at the effort of the vagabond Picts, saying "They can get their own tortoise shells." He and his men examined the damage. Their body language indicated they were not too upset. Four bundles had been taken. There were still twenty left. On the rest of the passage they insisted the party would only stop when required for the animals.

In Porto Bella, the party unloaded their wares on the British pier. Rambinder minded the horses and mules. Richards went to the Office to report on the activities, as expected.

"Some adventurers, my party. Passing through. The French are bringing in surveyors, land surveyors. The Dutch are looking for gold, as expected. The Norwegians are carrying in large saws. They say they'll cut down every tree in Panama and turn it into a desert."

"The Spanish?" asked the officer, Davies.

"None. Very quiet."

There was no need to report the robbery. Less chance his own hidden treasures would be discovered. Richards needs time.

"The Scots are on the prowl," Davies said. "I hear things are bad in New Edinburgh," He smiled and pulled an exquisite thin oak case out of his inside pocket. He made a show of extracting a wooden comb from the case. The teeth of the comb became longer and further apart along its length.

"This, was one of the combs the Scottish tried to trade with the Indians, 150 years ago." He brushed his beard with the low, tight end of the comb. He laughed a great laugh.

Davies family, from Durham, had made a fortune in the wool broker trade since Scotland lost its independence and joined England. They specialized in wool prepared for carpet making, and were selling internationally. It was pretty much by royal decree that the Scots had to sell their wares up the line, rather than directly to others. They also had to sell at a very reasonable price.

The Scottish attempt to colonize Panama in the early 1700s, and before, led to bankruptcy of its upper classes. They borrowed from the English in 1707 and signed away their independence as collateral.

One of Davies' great relatives had so much gold he even tried to build a castle.

It was a long laugh.

"The Americans do all their espionage in the taverns. This bloody place."

"On that sir. I must tell you I have to leave. I must get home. My leg is weak. I feel like a rat who must go home to die."

"Sorry to hear, Richards. Getting out of this stinkhole, for good, would do you a world of good. Too bad. I was going to ask if you wanted to do the same kind of work in Palestine. They have mules there too. The route to the Gulf of Aqaba. Great pay. May go myself."

"Too far, and too late for me I am afraid."

"This may play out. The problems in the Orient are on their first chapters I hear. Best to stay here."

The officer reached into a large nest of hemp rope coils hanging from a rafter and pulled out a bottle of Cuban rum.

"Guns and cannons are likely any day. Headed for Hong Kong. Ever been?"

"Was on my way. That's when I got jumbled."

John had a mangled leg, that's how he was able to get away from the service. They were loading in Bermuda and the net slipped, a barrel of oranges landed on his thigh and shattered it. They put his leg back together, but his left foot was twisted west by two fingers. It also let out small furious noises when he strains it.

He shifted his weight and his leg cracked three sharp notes.

He tapped his fingers on the top of a barrel. *Tappity-Tap-Tap.*

The officer poured them each a small rum. "Mare Liberum – to the free seas," they toasted.

JOHN RICHARDS gathered all his gear, including a bag of tradables, and headed for the market. He bought 120 pounds of Panamanian potting clay and had them pack it in ballast bags. He gathered some provisions – tack, mangoes, almonds, dried meat, coconut and two small barrels of water, along with a pistol, shot and powder, a tight ball of coca leaves, coconut mashed and soaked with yage, and a compass. He also bought a small brass bell.

A passing delivery of charcoal to the blacksmith caused him pause to consider getting a few silver ingots melted down. The smell of the furnace enticed him. He wanted to be near the fire. He wanted to watch the melt. But that was daft. There was no point. It would delay him. He couldn't spend it, and he didn't need anything else.

His leg was not good on the water. Standing, on a rocking boat, was inviting disaster. Sitting, the leg started to take on a spirit of its own. On a horse, the leg was fine. Bobbing in a boat it could lead to madness. The leaves and mash would take away the pain, and 'calm his toes'.

He enlisted a young lad with a handcart to carry his provisions. The young lad came with an assistant, a younger lad still.

They made their way through the tight lanes to the apron of the harbour, along the sharp smell of the town and the free smell of the sea. A small hand of piers for small boats fingered into the bay.

Richards stopped outside a rough shack. "Stay here," he said to the lads. "We'll be loading the sloop." He pointed towards an open boat, single sail, good for one man, best with two.

At the door to Denis Fontaine's shack, John paused to give his leg a rest. This should be his final tack.

"C'mon in, ya limp dick!" the Frenchman yelled. "I knows it's you out there. I can tell by yer hobble and bobble."

Richards opened the door and stepped inside. He kicked aside a net on the floor and shut the door.

The smaller lad sauntered up to the shack to give a listen. The young porter started to poke around the goods.

Denis was sitting on a three-legged stool, whittling a needle for nets.

"Denis, the day has come. I need the sloop," John announced.

"When?"

"Now."

"Such a hurry. I was going to do a run first light."

Denis drummed a bit on the edge of a barrel with the knife and needle.

"Need to make my way. Need to go home," John said.

"What's the hurry?"

"No hurry. No scurry. I must limp home, get back to my wheel."

Denis stopped his drumming, smiled a great smile and started again.

"Not for a season? Must have good reason. For good?"

"For good."

"You will take your sloop, named 'Logy Loop', never to return. I give it safe harbour, while you filled your larder, for this very day."

Denis changed rhythm.

"Your migration, puts this Haitian in a tight, tight, situation."

"You always have a situation, of your own provocation," John mirrored.

Denis laughed and stood up. "Aggravations! Time for tot?"

"No." Richards had to get going. The sun was low, the water soft. The Caledonians would be in town soon, with their news. Every low life in town would be looking for the jewels. Denis would be one of them.

A tumbling sound outside startled them. John opened the door, a ballast bag of the potting clay was half off the cart. The sound of the two boys running quickened, then faded.

"Rats," John said. "Denis, give me a hand loadin' up."

Nothing appeared to be missing.

Denis grabbed a lantern and went to assist. He handed it to John and carted the material to the sloop. John got on board and they began loading.

A large black sea dog walked up to the bags and clay and gave them a sniff. He made his way a few lengths along the pier and walked onto the boat, sitting in the bow.

"Salty wants to go home as well," Denis laughed. Salty was a St. John's water dog, who always sought out John when he was around.

"I'll take care of the pilot," Denis said. With that he waved the lantern three times. A light further up the harbour swung back twice. Denis waved the lantern three more times, then turned his back to the pilot and swung the lantern left to right, then back again, stopping the lantern directly in front, effectively turning out the light for the harbour pilot. He dimmed the light and turned. The pilot dimmed the distant marker.

"When you sell the Logy Loop in Havana – your destination I gauge - sell it to someone coming back here. She's the best wood I've sailed. A good dog should come home."

"She's comin' back to you, you crazy French buccaneer."

"I see you're going back to the potter's wheel," Denis said, nodding to the bags of clay.

"Aye," John said. "That's the plan."

"And I also see you carrying an English leather sack so tight in your coat, it looks like you are the King's purse."

John smiled. "My tools, my French friend. Half a craft is the tools of the craft. Send me on. Salty wants to go home." The dog's ears perked.

Denis untied the boat and gave it a gentle push with his foot. John raised the oars and dug them in the Atlantic, winching the vessel toward the abysse profond. Salty sat up and eyed the horizon. Dogs love adventures. Water dogs love going to work.

Sail raised, they slipped into the darkness, towards the infinity of stars.

On the water John prepared and tied a harness, with loose netting, around Salty. John Richards could not swim. If the boat should get capsized, he wanted to give chance a chance.

He also tied the bell around Salty's neck.

Fates
===

TWO SMALL BIRDS lit on the side of the sloop. They seemed to want to watch the sunrise. The Logy Loop was headed into busy waters.

A bird turned to John and said in the voice of his father – "You should be going through the Spanlish Channel, Jamaica to the west and Haiti to the east."

"Stay west of BirdShite Island – and go north-northwest to the sound of the bells," Richards said, recounting his father's directions, as recited when he had drawn the map on the large rock beside their home with the tip of a charcoaled stick. Salty was all ears.

The Jamaican Channel was the safest and most dangerous place in the Caribbean. Your fate was in the hands of those sailing her. All pirates. All points.

The other bird turned, and said in a woman's voice, "Your mother wants to know how your leg is doing. She is asking after you." It was his aunt, Rosemary, the third woman his father married, the woman who raised him.

"My leg is fine, mum. My linctus is strong."

"And your heart, John dear. How's your heart?"

Salty barked and all went quiet except the sound of the rising sun. RR3 turned to him and said "Hold on." The birds left their perch. Salty looked at John with sad eyes. His ears shifted their balance and the dog signaled to John to look at the growing sun, in fading light.

The ocean was boiling with life. Curtains of flying fish rose from the waters like a fountain. A wind of swordfish breached the water towards his boat. John dropped the sail and lifted the keel without thought to his action. The swordfish seemed to grow in

142

number as they flew closer. The sound of their exit and entry to the water gave way to a tremendous shudder.

Fish thumped against the side of the sloop. Salty and John lay low. Silver bellies streaked over the boat for at least the length of a short pipe. So many were falling into the boat, so fast, the Logy Loop was in danger of sinking like a stone. Salty started to kick them over the side between his legs, with great success. Then they stopped. John saw Salty freeze in the light of the rising sun, and fall into shadow, again.

He looked over the gunnel. Abeam to starboard a blue whale was breaching the water; its head and belly in the air; its tail leveraging the great mass above the sea. It was square to his tiny ship.

All light was eclipsed by the rising monster. As the whale dived, the world went blind.

A shock wave of water passed over the front of the sloop, taking Salty with it. A large swordfish hit the small mast broadside and landed on the bottom on the boat, its bill thrashing like a cutlass between John's legs.

The head of the whale slipped into the water so close to the boat John could count the colours of its skin. It would have hit the keel if it were still lowered.

The water whirl of the passing whale hardened the surface of the ocean. The whale's wake pushed the boat into the sky. John and the swordfish were pulled into the bottom of the boat.

The vessel ascended, stopped, suspended, and started to tilt. In freefall John exhaled; the business end of the swordfish floating inches from his guts.

The whale's tail caressed the gunnel. A backwave built and the water surface curved, the wake drawing the boat like a stone swung on a string into its rising center. The boat lay flat, the mast pointed directly at the eastern sun. The wave swept on and the boat began to freefall. The top fin of the swordfish snapped straight, catching the air. The Logy Loop landed, then righted by the following wave. The fish bounced between the gunnels and landed at John's feet.

The water went flat calm.

The Logy Loop creaked. John's leg echoed the creak with a crack-crack.

The swordfish began to stir.

John looked portside. No sign of Salty, or the whale. Or the bell. John needed the bell.

Then, the surface of the water rose, flattening further around the contour of the head of the whale as it breached. A shape on the crown emerged, and started to move.

The bell rang excitedly. Salty galloped towards the Logy Loop on the back of the great blue whale as it knuckled above the water.

John anchored his good foot near the tip of the swordfish's bill and grabbed its head. He managed to raise the beast's front, its body already elevated, straddling the center thwart.

The fish, out of water, realized it was under threat.

Salty, surely footed with webbed feet, ran up the tail of the whale as it arched high out the water. The dog reached the end of the tail as it snapped tack, launching Salty high in the air.

The furious sound of the clanging bell stopped.

The swordfish stiffened, giving John's hauling efforts greater sway. He could feel the fish rise some more.

Airborne, Salty curled into a ball.

The hoisting of the fish reached the apex. An angry critter when it snaps back to burden boards, John thought. Thank goodness Salty was near, and netted.

Salty hit the water, skipping along the surface of the sea.

John's leg cracked. The swordfish let out an eerie growl.

Salty slammed into the hoisted body of the great fish, knocking it out of John's hands, overboard. John fell deep into the stern.

Salty fell flat, and whimpered. The bell gave a slow 'ding-ding'.

The ocean boiled a second time as the earthquake moved through everything. John's leg exploded with pain.

Salty looked at John and said in his mother's voice, a voice he had never heard, "Watching out for you John. Watching out for you."

———◦———

John's mother kept on watching out for him. He made twelve chafing dishes while at Ira's and made it back to St. John's safely.

When you held the bottom of one of the dishes to the light, a silhouette of opals and silver disks appeared.

John Richards had two daughters and a son. Each inherited two of the jewel and silver encrusted platters. He broke two of the thinner dishes, and secretly converted the silver with a Norwegian trader.

The four remaining platters were donated anonymously to Bishop Fleming to help build the Basilica of St. John the Baptist on the hill. They covered a great deal of the cost of the construction.

One of John Richard's daughters was an ancestor to Michelle.

This was how her family came into possession the Spanish jewels, originally pirated by Captain Marion Thompson in 1821, and buried on Cocos Island in the Pacific. A great haul, some of the treasure was retrieved by Captain Keating and the Boag's 20 years later, and these prizes pilfered by John Richards in the jungles of Panama on their return.

Captain Keating met Captain Marion Thompson at a public inn in Matanzas, Cuba, in 1840. Thompson had been in hiding, was looking for a way to get back to England. Thompson presented himself as an able seaman, looking for work. Keating was a carpentry specialist aboard the Mercury, *doing trade between St. John's and Cuba. Fortunately, for Thompson, a key crew hand had died on the voyage down, and an experienced sailor was needed. Marion Thompson, a wanted man in every port in the world of the Spanish and the English, made his way back to St. John's. He had been hiding in Cuba for 20 years.*

Thompson became friends with Keating and drew him a map where the treasure of Lima was buried. Keating raised capital for an expedition from Avalon merchants. Captain Boag and his son, as insurance for the investors, accompanied Keating on the quest.

The trip was successful. Keating and the Boags made their way back to Panama from the secret treasured island in the Pacific. While they were waiting to sail from Panama, a small ferry they were all on capsized and the elder Boag was eaten by sharks. His arm was the only part of him ever found, and is buried in Panama City.

Captain Marion Thompson, one of the original thieves of the Spanish jewels, wanted to get to St. John's to hook up with Lord Cochrane, Commander-in-Chief of the Royal Navy North American Station. Lord Cochrane had taken a portion of the Lima treasure in 1821. One man was the most wanted man in every port, and the other had the final word in many a British station.

In San Francisco, a failed writer, far adrift from his home in England, drinking in harbourside shacks, heard accounts, as told by working seamen, of Thompson's adventures of buried gold. Robert Louis Stevenson penned Treasure Island based on these tales.

Stevenson fared much better than Thompson, Keating, and John Richards. And Oscar Wilde.

Lord Cochrane held his own.

Keating had the infamous map that Stevenson imagined. He had lived just down the street from where Tony was born, by Ed Kelly's uncle's place, next to the boarding house where James McGregor stayed. That area has been burned to the ground a few times.

Robert Louis Stevenson had slept at an inn on the same street, when he first made his way to San Francisco, and his ship took on supplies in St. John's.

Bloodstone

"JONES, half this load is not acceptable" the lead stonemason said to the beleaguered quarryman.

Jones was tired. Fourteen cartloads of slate, quarried, loaded on ship, unloaded on the harbour and brought up this mighty hill. All he wanted was to get dry, and some sleep.

"The stone is fine, good sir. The pieces are exceptionally large, the grandest I have ever cut."

The stonemason walked over to the first cart, and made a showing of turning over a large slag piece, the height of a dog.

"See. See here." He did not bother pointing. "The stone face is covered with squished fish, flattened flounder, and hideous halibut. We can't put this in a church."

Jones ran his fingers across the fossils. "They are beautiful. These forms have not seen the light of day since the great flood. They are truly biblical."

The mason was not impressed. "Aye. I know why they call their source Mistaken Point. You are mistaken if you think these grotesques will adorn the walls of the basilica. A dungeon, maybe. A refuge for tormented souls, perhaps. But not the house of God. Not on my watch."

"I suggest you bring it up with the Bishop. Ten carts of slate I was to supply. Fourteen have been delivered. My work is done."

Jones had already been paid.

The Bishop had sought him out months before. He heard Jones was a quarryman in Panama, returned to Newfoundland to take care of his family, his ailing mother and sickly sister. He came by Jones' house in Renews in late May, by sloop from St. John's, unannounced.

148

The Bishop was full of questions. Known acquaintances? Names of ships? Frequent travellers from Newfoundland? Questionable men of the sea passing through Panama, certainly a naive enquiry.

"I'm no pirate your eminence. I cut stone. My family is not warm to the water." The Bishop was getting annoying. Why would anyone make the trip from St. John's to Renews to ask a few questions?

Suspicious characters in Panama. Big spenders. Charitable fellows?

"All the Newfoundlanders I knew in Panama were dogs. Newfoundland dogs. We used them in the quarry. One fellow, a mute, named Dicks, from Harbour Grace I believe, would buy our old dogs, for work in the port, the Scottish port."

The Bishop smiled. He asked if Jones was looking for work. He offered him a contract for stone from the Southern Shore, the best slate the quarryman could find. Ten large carts.

Jones accepted the contract. He knew just the stone, the living rock on the point.

Jones figured the Bishop would never put together that Dicks was really Richards, that the mute fellow was really lame, that the port was really a trail through the jungle. It was a safe distance from the truth. Jones could repeat it with certainty. It seemed to stop the Bishop's queries.

There was no longer a Scottish port. Jones had to leave a clue. The quarry was the only part of the tale that was square. Jones worked the quarry in Panama for several years, and came home when he was rich.

"You are a good man, Mr Jones. And to show the noble faith of the Church, you will be paid now for your labour, before you swing a pick." The Bishop took a leather purse from inside his frock and let some silver slide onto the rough table, four British coins. He jostled the bag a bit more. A blank ingot and a large opal rolled out.

Jones didn't flinch.

The bishop returned the silver ingot to the purse. He picked up the opal, and set it atop three fingers. "For the cross on the altar Mr Jones. What is your opinion, Mr Jones, of this gem?"

The stone was almost as large as the ones Jones had taken from the Scottish wildman, after he bashed his head with a sledgehammer.

Jones reached out and grasped Bishop Fleming's outstretched hand by the wrist, and moved it towards the crack in the curtain veiling the window. The transparent rock focused the light of the low sun and the room was bathed in a soft, turquoise spirit.

"If blood could stain rock your eminence, all jewels would be deep red. I am a simple man of stone. Others can have their shiny things."

The Bishop opened his fingers and let the stone slide into the palm of his hand. "If you ever hear of Mr Dicks, or any of his family, be so kind to let me know Mr Jones."

The bishop nudged the British coins across the table.

"I will. Your humble servant. You will have your slate for your grand church. Aye, it will stand till the end of time; as god is my witness."

With one hand he scooped the coins, with the other he fingered the curtain open, revealing a small, chiselled statue of the Black Christ of Portobello, a weight for his papers.

Red shift from street stones

Found on Beth's phone

Livingstone Homestead – 92% Diane filter

Rock, Paper

[Perfectly matched fields in father-son pairing. Such a strong
pattern produces a foundation layer for other extractions.]

Cut the music

"WHEN YOU WERE LITTLE you had baby root beer?" Bud
asked.

"Yes. They brought it to the car. On a tray. It
hooked on the window. Every second Sunday me
and Pop and Nan would come here and I would have baby root
beer and fries. Just like you," Leonard said.

"That's a lot. Every second Sunday. We never come here." Bud
took a slurp of his root beer.

"This was the only fast food place in town," Leonard said. "Now
there are four or five places to go." Bud knew them all, and was
good at spotting them from his car seat.

"I'm five," Bud stated. "I'll be six in Sep-em-burr."

"We will try to make it out here once a year. I promise," Leonard
said.

A pair of women, Leonard's age, sat at the table next to them. The
one in the sweater twinkled her fingers at Bud. "Cutie pie" she
whispered.

The women arranged the food off their trays. "There seems to me
more wreaths this year," the sweater girl said, wiping her face
with a napkin, even though she had not eaten anything.

Two more wreaths Leonard figured. The fisherman's kids must be
all grown up. Probably they moved into town. He had just came
back from the site a few minutes ahead of the women. Maybe they

were driving into town. He had to pass it, turn around and come back.

He was home. Just watched the national news and had a typical low voltage seizure because they were all over Canada Day on the news, but didn't mention Memorial Day at all. It was like one of the key days of remembrance in Newfoundland was being ignored. They always had their Dominion Day and we always had our Memorial Day. Confederation never changed that. But now it was Canada Day. All Canada Day. Some fireworks. Concerts. Television ads for rakes.

And to top it off there was speculation that there was going to be an announcement tomorrow about the fishery. It had been suggested the feds were going to shut it down. After 500 years of fishing. It's like turning off nature. How could you shut down a fishery? "Shut down banks. Insurance companies," he had yelled at the television. Fisherman from all parts of the province were coming into town.

Noelle had left to help her friend Cheryl. Cheryl and Howard lived out in da Pearl.

Howard was acting up again. Howard lost his legs below the knees - a minefield in Kuwait - and the ads for weed killer probably sent him well past Leonard's sense of indignation. Military guys liked their liquor, but there's only so much pain you can bottle up.

The phone rang. At 11:30 pm. Who calls at 11:30 pm? The baby was asleep.

"I'll never forget it," the non-sweater gal said. She was on the same side of the table as Leonard, and he never really got a good look at her. She was wearing a light blazer, changed somehow, but it still looked like an outfit from Miami.

The sweater gal picked up her soft drink, she was going to have to listen to it again this year.

"We were coming up behind the tractor trailer. Full of oil pipes it was. Burf said 'Whoa' as the truck just swerved on Kenmount Road without slowing down. I thought I saw the pickup on the side of it as we approached, but I can't really be sure. We slowed down. There was a massive crack sound. Then the pickup was under the rear wheels of the big truck. The big truck started to turn over. All those pipes. The pickup was there crumpled. Behind, there was a streetlamp. We saw it shake. That's when the car hit the pole. I remember watching as the globe from the streetlamp fell in slow motion. Sparks everywhere. Then the car glanced back on the road. In the air it hit a transport truck that was trying to avoid the pickup." She made a spinning motion with her hand, finger pointed down to the table. Bud was playing a small sword fight with two french fries. "The car hit the truck in the grill." She punched the air with her fist. "And the car - on fire - flew over the pickup and exploded." Fingers outstretched. "The second big truck went off the road. It was full of stuff for the Regatta. Plush toys... soaked in glycol. Giant bags of popcorn seed spilled everywhere."

Bud stopped playing with his french fries. Perhaps it was hearing the word 'toys'. Perhaps it was popcorn. His Dad hated popcorn. He stared at the lady.

She kept on going, with a lower voice.

"Burf sort of hit me, trying to slow the car down. I had a miscarriage, apparently. Lucky it must have been twins. The lefties always survive."

"You think that caused the miscarriage? I thought you were headed to the hospital anyway."

"That's what I told Burf. He caused the miscarriage." She took a nibble of her burger. Bud fisted some more fries.

"Then all the police and ambulances showed up. Seemed like two minutes. We parked and looked. There was nothing we could do for anyone. Burf was just released from Dorchester. He wanted to stay low. They went right to the car, the firemen, with the Jaws of Life. And I never told you this before - the two firemen, they did a 'Rock, Paper, Scissors' between them to see who would operate the Jaws of Life. There was no point. No hurry. The fire just kept popping up. The car was so beaten up all the wheels had been knocked off. You couldn't tell if it right side up or upside down."

"The firemen just do that. The senior fireman always wins. He plays scissors. The other guy plays paper. They just do it. Teamwork, command thing," the sweater gal said. "I remember that from when I worked Emerge. Firemen are a bit odd."

"C'mon Bud. Let's go," Leonard gently suggested.

"Maybe the firemen put up a wreath this year," Miami gal said.

"Wreaths!" Bud piped up. "We saw wreaths. They are for my mom," he said. "She died when I was little. In a car crash. In a car." He slapped his little hands together. "Always wear your seatbelt," he advised.

Leonard did not know whether to feel ashamed, proud or sad. There would always be a numbness. A part of his heart was gone, forever.

He looked into the space in between the others. "That's the night the music died."

For most people that was the day the rock had been papered over. Bureaucracy erased geography. For Leonard it was the day he became untethered, cut from the world. God left his life. Now his life was Bud, and for the time being, he was Bud's.

156

The following day, the Canadian federal Minister of Fisheries announced the moratorium on the Newfoundland cod fishery, under British based colonial watch for close to 500 years. It is considered one of the worst man made ecological disasters of the 20th century.

People were not pleased.

Type: Notice - Read once

From: NF7717044

Subject: NF8528887 In

Incoming audio. Will be released after analysis.

Current Correspondence

From background radio signals found in many samples

Riding the Wave

[Node cluster from initial sequence, required as a harmonising branch, and as ballast for main payload.]

Nurture

FIONA WAS NOT A HUGE FAN of the Grim Reaper Cafe. It wasn't that the cafe is in a former funeral home. It wasn't because the cafe was across the street from the dirty prison. Fiona wasn't a big fan of the Grim Reaper Cafe because there were always some odd lesbians around. Odd in the sense they were hard-nosed end-of-roaders, wanting to get as far away as possible from their home town somewhere on the mainland, or liberal arts refugees from the states somewhere. They didn't even hang out with the local lesbians. Just as well.

Fiona had nothing against lesbians. She has little time for assholes.

These come-from-away lesbians tended to congregate here under Signal Hill. Some had burrowed into homes around here. A side street was referred to as "LickaMaid Lane." Some went for walks around the lake or up on the hill. They always looked like they were putting on a show that no one was watching.

Her aunt, who died of cancer, and who was waked in this very room where Fiona now waited for a Pumpkin Creme Cappuccino and a slice of banana bread, took up walking around the lake after she was first diagnosed.

The lake, Quidi Vidi, was below the prison. Fiona had a good view of the prison, but not the lake. Fiona heard if people walked around the lake clockwise, it meant they were battling cancer. If counter-clockwise, they considered their cancer beaten. She imagined wry smiles and small tears as walkers passed in the fog, exchanging "See you tomorrows."

Her aunt, Gloria, hardly got to know the footpath around the pond.

Fiona had wanted to get here early, to have half an hour for a bowl of soup, and to clear her head. She had to digest the inevitable pain of her aunt's memory before meeting with Tony and Bud, a pain pinned to location and stored in her memory set as one of her "Places of Sad Memories".

Gloria was her mother's only sibling. The wake, in this room, was quite a few years ago. Fiona was only 5 or 6. She remembers it as being underwater, as she was small and below the levels where everyone talked. She spent most of the time near her Nan, her mother's mother, or trying to play with her sister, Rebecca.

Rebecca is three years older. Fiona has always figured that her sister and her dad held something against her, as Mary, her mother, died shortly after giving birth. Fiona lived with the guilt of thinking she was a 'demon-child', whose first act in the world was to kill her loving adoring mother; until four years ago when her Father, a few days before he dropped dead, told her Mary had died from an infection that was probably from a dental procedure, completed a few days before her birth.

Rebecca of course didn't believe Fiona when she shared their dad's account of their mother's death. She didn't want to accept it, Fiona figured, as Rebecca had used their mothers' passing as a foundation layer for her inherent superiority over her little sister. Rebecca had no real memory of her mother's death, not even the funeral. She was only three and a half.

In her early years Rebecca found herself spending a lot of time with her younger sister, a vibrant child who could quickly give rise to smiles and laughter. The star of the show who killed her mother, was saying a dental hygienist having a bad day, took her Mamma, the only person in the world who ever loved her; who could ever love her.

In the imagined arc of her own story, Fiona knows she lost her sense of funny, her timing, her drive to get an audience to love her, right after she heard this news from her father. The only adult she figured who could corroborate her father's account was his sister Julia, and she was on the South Coast of the island.

You don't just drop by the South Coast, it's an excursion. Fiona could get to Dublin or Havana in less time it would take to get to the South Coast. Hell, she'd be ready to return rested from any of those places before she crossed her Aunt's threshold with 4 liters of fresh milk that her Aunt might not open, less she get used to the taste. She would feed the milk to the cats and the dogs.

Her father never remarried. He had several girlfriends, and Fiona had heard her aunt say he quickly closed off all his relationships 'for the girls'. All except one, Barbara. Barbara was much younger than her dad. A striking, dark brunette with coils of hair. She was in the Armed Forces and moved to Ottawa about a year after they started to see each other. Her dad went up after her for a few days, and when he came back it was like his adrenalin glands had been removed. Nothing could excite him anymore.

Her father not telling Fiona how her mother died, until he was falling into the grave, made Fiona 'who she was', her Dad said. She 'needed it' he added, being the smallest in the truncated family.

There were quite a few things her father said to her over the years that stuck with her.

"It's important to think big. Anyone can live big."

"Know what you are thinking. Change tracks when you need to. Train yourself to change tracks."

'Tracks' was a common theme in her Dad's philosophy of life. He said research showed people generally thought of 16 different things at any given moment. Their consciousness was comprised of these 16 separate tracks of thought, he figured.

"The tracks change with age. As an adult you think about your surroundings - what's the food situation, do I have a warm place to shit. Then you think about the people around you. Are you safe? Can you help? There is a track for the people you love, the people in your family. There's work. Current events. Personal interests. A sport or two. The people you like. The people who like you. New things. Old things. That about does it."

Then he'd throw in one of a handful of corollaries.

- "That's why junk television is evil. It gets in there."
- "That's why pelicans have it so easy. People just want them to go away, so they pay no attention to politics." He called politicians pelicans for some reason.
- "You need to clean the heads. That's what vacations are all about. And fly fishing."

The Pumpkin Crème Cappuccino would hopefully clean her heads so she could change tracks with whatever Bud had come up with. She may get out of this seasonal gulag, she hoped. Failed expectations test the measure of faith, and her faith was worn thin. In the East, the Far East, people wish to shed so they can be free. Fiona was letting hope go, all she had left.

The two lesbians sitting at the best situated table by the bay window ramped up the volume on a private conversation into a public fight. The larger one grabbed her knapsack and moved out of the bench like a frightened seal, yelling "Go. Just go. Go." She stood and took two twenties out of her pocket and made a show of wrapping them around her conjoined middle and ring fingers.

She thrust out her hand and gave her companion a double middle finger, wagging the face of the Queen. Her offending hand turned and the fingers splayed so the money fell on the table. "Take your goddamn china and yoga mat and go back to Timmins," she said.

Fiona's head was clear. Empty. The café filled with blurred patches of yellow light, a reflection from a passing chrome yellow Lotus.

Livingstone Homestead, along trail, from found metal

AFTER TONY AND FIONA LEFT Bud penned the date and "DCC" on the back of the receipt. He took pictures of the front and the back, and entered the notes and pictures in an Accounting ledger on his phone.

This was something Bud learned in school. The institution specialized in "Life Skills". It wasn't a basic skills curriculum to assist the not-so-bright. It promoted that high achievement can only be reached with an appreciation for experience and excellence in simple tasks, like cooking, budgeting, scheduling, having a meeting or debate. The approach was meant to promote group approaches to problem solving.

Everyone was expected to draw up budgets and keep track of every cent they ever made and every cent they ever spent. The first two years this was part of a one hour class, three days a week. The next year it was half an hour, and in the last everyone spent 15 minutes with a counsellor every week to go over their finances.

Cooking was a blast. Everyone rotated through groups of five students and they would cook for each other, the class, the grade, soup kitchens, seniors, and fundraising events. Bud still knows how to prepare triple chocolate pecan cookies for 200 hungry kids.

Prospective job applicants have the "Kitchen Grill" thanks to graduates from Bud's alma mater - *The Geraldine Mary School of Names.* In the Kitchen Grill (called "Let's Make a Meal" on the west coast) interviewees were brought into an unfamiliar kitchen and asked to prepare a meal they thought appropriate. This job interview tested how people reacted, how they multitasked, their manners and cooking skills. Some simply took some beer out of the fridge and opened a bag of chips. Others took the opportunity to make a free, welcome, lunch.

Geraldine Mary founded the institution on the lost philosophy of the Chinese School of Names. These dialecticians dabbled in the metaphysics of words and their meaning, helping name ideas in China 2,500 years ago. Their teachings and practise were either purposely eradicated or accidently misplaced, in the smoke of history. They were surrealists, showing weaknesses in sets of symbols. Languages had different meanings when spoken or written. The idea changed in the context of delivery. It was absolutely possible that "A white horse is not a horse," in the constructs of Chinese thinking and writing. You can think of a horse, and talk about a horse. But when you write about a horse the idea is neither clear, nor unique. It was easy to mistake a written horse, white in colour, as a champion of peace in time of conflict. The horse was no longer a horse. It became an idea.

As part of her doctoral study, Geraldine Mary imagineered how the philosophers of the Chinese School of Names would design a curriculum for young people in the 20th century. At its core was a discussion around what it means to "teach," to "learn," and to "train". It asked what education should give its students, and the answer was extremely simple - "To get by, remarkably." In Latin *"Impetro per, ingens"*

The concept took off in the Scandinavian countries, and Geraldine Mary build her own private school overlooking the harbour of Torbay. She started with only 75 students. The spots were snapped up by Norwegians and Swedes holed up on the mini-estates in the woods on the northern Avalon Peninsula, directly north of the city of St. John's airport. The locals thought it was some kind of school of special advantage and clamoured to have their children enrolled. The rumour was even the French were taking their kids out of French immersion to attend the School of Names.

Bud translated the motto on his phone once, it came back as "To get really, huge."

Livingstone Homestead, memory stick

BUD SHOWED Fiona and Tony the bank statement. They had $165,000 in the bank. They had 50 performances, pre-sold. They would have an opening two week run, with a week break, a four week run, then another week break with another four week run. With ten shows a week, this was 100 shows, meaning they could bring in a quarter of a million dollars in ten weeks. There was a clause in the contracts that the sponsors could extend their underwriting, if they wanted.

"Once the word gets out that people can go to a show for free we have to make it happen. Buses, pickups, valet parking, whatever it takes to get people to the theatre."

They had to have an ordered, open concept, drawing on all kinds of talent. Colleen would be the Business Manager for the project. He outlined the program:

Monday
- off
Tuesday
- Seniors targeted shows, a noontime and early matinee.
Wednesday
- Armed Services focused. Early cabaret followed by in house band and dance.
Thursday
- Comedy shows, early and late night.
Friday
- Talk Show based talent show, work towards a television deal.
Saturday
- Kids workshops in the morning, matinee children's show, with a late night cabaret.
Sunday
- Seniors workshops, RomCom matinee, no evening show.

He shared the roster of people who had their tickets prepaid by a generous sponsor.

- Seniors
- Military

- Children under 14
- Police and their families
- Retired Teachers
- Families of long term or hospice care
- Norwegians
- Spa customers (2 separate sponsors)
- Health conventions
- Families of residents of three Seniors facilities
- Families in one of four newly created suburbs
- Plumbers and Pipefitters
- People with Tourette's (special cabarets planned, web event in the works)
- Families of people working offshore
- Registered fisherfolk

Bud explained there were more sponsors available, but he had to stop after four days; the pot was full. The goal was a month but he pushed it out to 10 weeks. The net broadcast talk show would help pay for some premium talent, and the web material would support the works.

"We are going to put cameras everywhere. On set. In the audience. Drones. Dressing rooms. Might build a confession booth. People are going to be able to tune in to whatever they want. We will have a couple of content mixers, and people will be able to watch streams put together by others."

"Everyone will get paid. Paid well, rates or more," Bud said. Then he counted off. "If we get some seniors, who were in the military, living in one of those condos up in BlackWater, with Tourette's - we could count that as 4 seats. Five if they visit the spa."

Tony turned to Fiona. "Guess we'll have to quit the 'Troubles'."

"Gladly," she said.

"The only people who will definitely have to pay are students." Bud shrugged. "I tried. No one cares about students."

From civic dump, Witless Bay area

Balance

TONY REMEMBERED the first time he was 'on skates'. He had been on skates a few times before, but these efforts were full of missteps. Fitted, new skates, with tighter boots gave him confidence. He noticed how much taller he was, an inch and a half is a measure of age for a six-year-old. He shifted his weight to his back foot and raised the other. He pushed himself into a controlled fall. His lead foot glided on the ice, and he followed. His back foot lifted and landed, creating a new vector. He could skate. He saw what the older kids were doing - turning, stopping, going backwards - and knew he could do all these. His pendulum of slowly falling, and gliding, had kicked in. This is how he would move forward the rest of his life, falling and gliding, riding the wave.

Defining Moments – Leonard

Buttons

SHE WALKED UP THE STAIRS and into Leonard's house, stopping in the doorway. Diane was wearing a red beret with a tiny silver pin. The high bright upturned yellow collar on the dark green tartan canvas raincoat accentuated her neck and cheekbones. Her arms were crossed, her hands loosely holding black leather gloves. At the waistband of the coat, where you may expect a belt, a large square of fabric - the size of an outstretched hand - extended across, terminated by two crimson buttons. Her legs, in straightcut jeans, were crossed. Her boots cut at mid-calf with a stylized upper suede trim.

"Listen. I am not sure if I am ready for a relationship."

Leonard smiled.

"I like it. I like being in a relationship."

Leonard tried not to move.

"I'm really good at it. It fits me. It locks me in. Of all the highs I have ever had, being in a simple relationship is the best."

Leonard managed a nod. A small nod.

A slight shock snapped through Diane's frame. She uncrossed her legs.

"There's more now in a relationship. A good relationship. Your life is bigger just by being with them. Your past makes sense. Your future has hope."

She raised her hands, moving coils of time.

171

"The future should become a continuation, an improvement, of your past. Some people want the future to be different than their past. That's tough. That takes a lot of work."

Leonard wondered *'Is she ever going to fucking say anything about me?'*

"But if the relationship stops. If someone quits…"

Leonard to self - "*Fuck. Here it comes….*"

"I'm devastated. I'm broke. It takes a long time to heal. And I don't want to spend any more time healing."

Leonard to self – "*I'm just standing here. I am not a fucking Ebola virus.*"

"Do you want to change your future?"

Finally, a trick question. Leonard spoke.

"I have enough difficulty with the present, b…" He cut himself off from saying 'babe'. It can be a real conversation-ender.

He continued "The future at best is a six month horizon. In fact, the real future is as many days as I can count on my fingers and toes. The future will just be the same; the same size, the same problems. If you want a change you can achieve some small change in 6 months. And then you can do some more. Some change is good. Most change happens elsewhere."

He shifted his weight, intending to take a step.

Diane smiled. "You sure? Will you remember that?"

"You bet." There was no seam on the shoulder of her jacket. The material was a single piece of tailored oilcloth. The buttons on the coat changed colour. All became white.

"Next time, you say Hi." Diane turned and walked out the door.

From fabric found at Livingstone Homestead

Beads

THE NURSE REACHED into the pocket of her frock and pulled out some rosary beads. Diane was lying on the large king bed in the master bedroom. Leonard sat beside her. Some home care ephemera stood parked on the bedside table.

The nurse, from Labrador City, was good at home care. She picked up Diane's wrist, then laid it down. She held a small mirror up to Diane's nose and mouth.

"She's gone, Mr Livingstone, I'm sorry to say."

She offered Leonard the beads. Some like to fold the arms and place the beads in the hands, for when others arrived.

Rain smashed against the windows and skylights.

Leonard shook his head, declining the offer. He reached out for the small mirror, the last record of Diane's life.

"This is all No," he said. "This is most real thing I have ever seen." He looked at the mirror. The chiseled face of his youth was worn. He was alone.

Extracts

[These extracts are a common layer across all subjects, but may exhibit a significant bias on the Leonard Livingstone vector. Samplings were deliberately abbreviated, due to tendency for views in these fields to slip outside rational, formative structure. The institute is still recovering from the unrestrained flows released by the Murphy cluster, and hopes to cap the release in the near future. We have learned from our mistakes.]

Life and Death

THE MESSAGE BETWEEN THINGS IS LIGHT. The message is always the same, "Things have changed." The message creates time. Time only moves in one direction, and is the collective act of things seeing the light, reading the messages, sensing change.

We are a collection of things, of cells arranged in organs, very adept at seeing the change around us. We reproduce so other versions of ourselves - our children, our half-lives so to speak - can make more changes, can make things better. We use light to make things better.

Then we stop. Our cells break down. Our mind, the ability to see the changes, no longer has a single channel. We are no longer aware that things are changing.

We live. We see and make changes. We die.

But parts of us live on. Our children live on. People who carry our light live on. The changes we made are enhanced by others. The conversations we start are continued. We are and we are not. Because you think, I am.

You think therefore I am.

Death is the great equalizer. But we do not know what it means to be dead.

Dead person plural – there is no tense in our language for such a state.

People who believe they know what it is like to be dead usually have a very narrow view of what it is like to be alive.

We imagine death is a good thing. We hope death is good.

We live in hope. We build stories of hope. We give these to our children, it makes it easier for them. When we give our stories, we give a bit of ourselves to others.

Others tell our stories, keep our light.

Hopes can change. Everything can change.

The News

THE NEWS IS VERY IMPORTANT. It is information. The news is like the planets, in different orbits.

At the center is the Sun, the stories we all agree upon. Here lies stories of love, compassion, and kindness. The stories of Death also live on the Sun. These stories illuminate our lives.

Around the Sun flies Mercury. These are the tales of Heroes. And Villains. Here lies the stories of the great struggle between Life and Death.

Then we have Venus. Our interpretation of the stories where we find comfort keep this orbit. These are our dreams, our successes. They are close.

Next is ourselves. Our own messy little world, cycling between abundance and labour camps of despair. Our memories of what we know to be true, these shifting tides, circle us.

A bit further out is the conflict around us, our warring neighbours. We hear a lot of these stories.

Then it's a gasball of ephemera. Narratives that feel alien to us. We can't keep track of all the moving pieces. They are native to different roots.

Then we have the stories from our history. The refined stories. Perfect alignment of elements that set a standard.

There is a collection of stories we will never understand, never even hear. They fly unnoticed in grand arcs.

The tales of the assholes of the world are in the next orbit. They are far out in the cold, well past most of the other information we have before us. But they help bring balance and order.

And then we have the place for the tales of our departed. The largest part of our unknown universe. They race ahead, not able to tell us what they see.

Blink, there is a new star. Something changed.

William Shatner @WilliamShatner · Apr 20
I have a drinking problem...I'm addicted to water. 😜

Reconstructed from radio signals; Binary Recovery Unit – Fogo
Facility

CREATING A LAW should not be confused with creating a god. People who sit in judgement must own their decisions. To say a judgement is in agreement with some imaginary, metaphysical, cannot-be-experienced-by-design god, is simply lame. It is a cop-out. It is cheap.

People must own their decisions. But what happens when people decide to hurt others? Nobody wants this. It has to be corrected. To be corrected, the group must decide to hurt the person doing the hurting. This requires some clever logic. Hurting now becomes conditional. This can make love conditional as well. This is a fall from grace.

There are three parties - the perpetrator, the crowd, and the court selected by the crowd to stop the perpetrators. The perp hurts the crowd. The court hurts the perp. Person hurts, person gets hurt. The bad forces hurt the crowd, and the good forces hurt the bad. Balances out.

But where does it start and where does it end? What happens when the crowd sees the court punish someone who has not yet hurt the crowd? What happens when that hurt is an idea? What happens when the crowd likes the idea?

In steps God. The court say they are doing it on behalf of God. God handed them a manual. "Do It Yourself God." First step, say the law is God's idea. Second step, defend the first step no matter what. You can always use the first step to justify the second step. So it will be a long struggle, over generations, so there needs to be a good backstory.

Then everyone dips into prehistory. Which means none of us know what happened. So we plant little god stories in this garden of imagination. It is a field of laws and gods chasing truth and logic. At some point, it gets written down.

Or sometimes the idea is God. A person will tell people about God and the crowd will like the idea. The court may not like the idea and punish the man. This is the Jesus story.

Logic is not a threat. Truth is not the enemy. Stop making things up.

Selfie, NF8528887

GOVERNANCE is often dependent on who it sees as a power higher than itself. It looks in a mirror and stares. It cuts its hair, brushes its teeth. It works on the profile, for the medals it yearns to hand out. It asks for assistants and many volunteer, many with a lifelong commitment to this set of rules.

So is anyone surprised when governance becomes a parody of itself? Its backstory is confusing. There are different accounts of the early years, the lean years, when perfection, from keen innocence, was formed.

"We do, however, have pictures of all the members of the board. And paintings, we go back that far."

God is simply the people older than us, ones born before us. Eternal life is the young among us, born after we saw what we saw.

How do you fix governance, or at least have the peace of mind to believe it is being watched? Teach. Learn. Teach the children, especially the young girls. Learn from your elders. The hard part here is you have to ask them questions to get their attention. They have a lot on their mind. They see themselves as further from the shore than you. At least pretend to be interested.

Let the young take care of it. But do your part.

Truth and Logic

IT'S ALL ABOUT the relationship between our ideals and the real variations that make up the ideal. The relationships change with no observer, a single observer, and multiple observers.

A single person can believe whatever they want. They can believe their own take on something is the ideal point of view, the standard. Their own logic confirms it. They provide their own measure.

Many people have to apply a common reasoning to the idea. The variations become fewer. Standards are set. The logic is recorded. Everything is measured.

Is a meter a meter if there is no one there to measure it? The measure is all that exists with no observer, one can say, if one could be around to say it.

Some of these ideals are the same for all. The case of 'no observer' being a thought experiment. It is a test of the logic. These ideals are truths. Everything else is a shitshow. It is survival of those who make the best guess.

If we are not here, can truths be tested?

When things are unknown, there are many possible answers. When we look, we derive an answer.

PEOPLE ARE ATTRACTED to shiny things. Always have been. Always will be. Power is about controlling all the shiny things - the gold, the silver, and the blades of war. Some people need to feel in control, of everything. They will do anything to get in power.

And politics is the art of keeping people in power. It is the usher that will not let you see behind the curtain.

Cited as a noble service, politics is a ceremonial attempt at sharing.

The people we vote for are all part of a ceremony. They take care of some shiny things.

But politics only takes care of a few of the shiny things. It issues tokens, as a gesture of sharing. The other shiny things are distributed to other groups, mostly families, or representatives of families.

Those people have the power. We live in their turbulence. This cannot be changed.

The best shiny thing is a mirror. Test your truths while there is still light.

Relationships

THEY ARE COMPLICATED, undeniable and use a lot of your personal fuel. There are people you just need to be with, and those you do not want in your orbit.

Knowing which ones to concentrate on can be difficult. There is only so much time. Quickly, your dependence on others can become invisible. So, check their fitting before they bind around you, and you around them.

Personal, loving relationships take on many forms, by many degrees.

Relationships can be measured by your arm. The people you want close, within reach, add a lot to your life. Many times there is an undeniable chemical reaction. Smells and tastes are heavily involved. You can be with someone and they simply spice up your life. You feel that unique experience, through your body, which feels good. People write a lot of songs about how it feels good.

A taste sensation, an active umami, the person who adds mustard to your life, is very captivating. No matter what you think of the person, one smell, one visual clue, one tone of voice, and all your defenses ease. Comfort.

Shelf life, different story.

The people you don't like, you tend to keep more than an arm's length away. Some, you'd like to take a swing at. Get them out of the way. Every enemy has a price. No conflict is cheap. You need to have a plan if you want to remove someone from your life. There are always consequences, casualties. Practicalities need to be considered.

This is hard enough on a personal level. On a group level, hating is much easier than loving. The benefits of not having some people around is that there is probably more for you, and the ones close to you. Even threatening not to have them around has very good benefit, as others can be made to do a lot of work you would rather not do. It's quite tempting, as a group, to agree that another group's proper place in life is to clean up your shit. It's also tempting on a personal level. Boss and assistant couplings have a very permanent bond. Empires work on this premise, this lopsided dependency.

Now, we have great range. We can poke at our enemies from a distance, and they can rain terror on us.

On a personal level we can tap away into the ether, irritating others. On a group level, there is great danger.

We have the capability to more or less wipe everyone out, if things get out of hand, as they tend to do, when nations go full batshit crazy on one another.

Under these conditions, death itself is a thought experiment. Everyone can be killed. Just because we are not pushing the button does not make us saints.

Life is also a thought experiment. Choose your lab partners wisely.

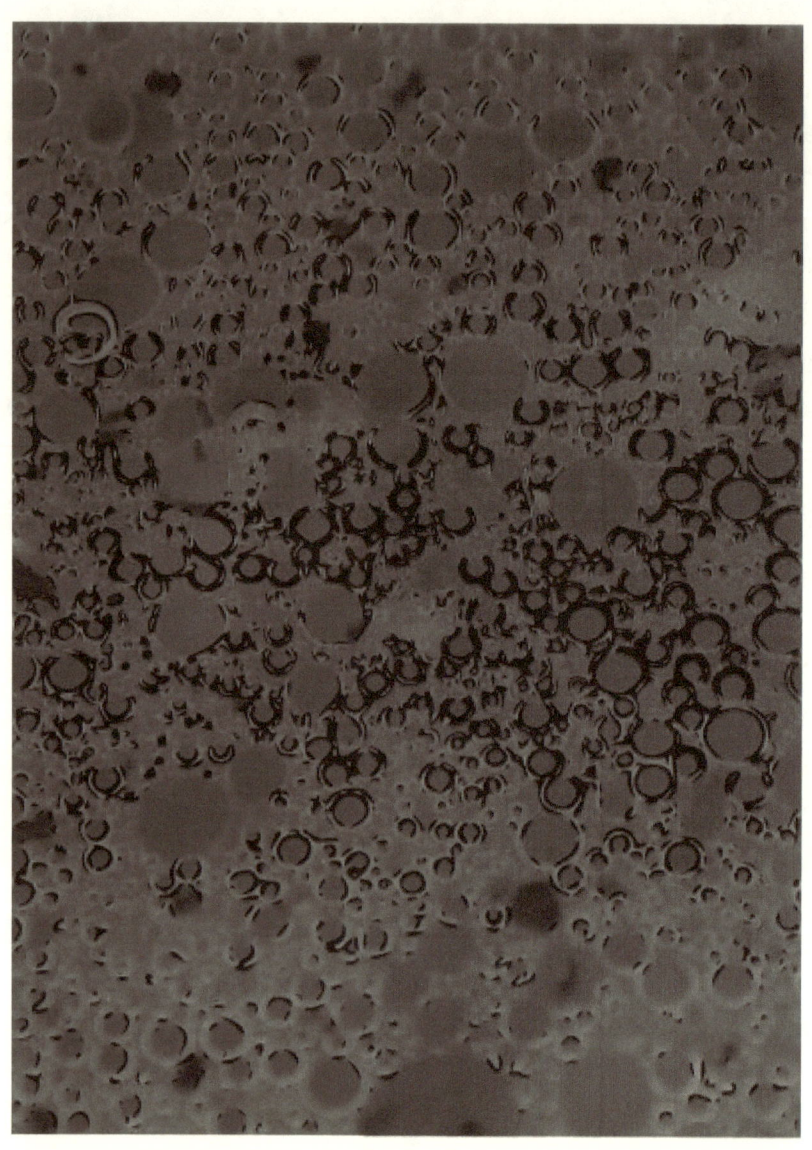

Universe cluster activity, near event; Mageotronics LLM

Water of Life

[Keystone threads.]

Aqua Vitae

A T THE CREST OF THE PATH, looking back past the curve of the hill, Leonard could see the silhouette of Ed Kelly's house in the belly of the contrary hill. The back porch light was on, on the side opposite. It was around 8:30 pm, Ed Kelly's high noon. He should be bar-be-queing, working on his Harley, or building some energy saving whirlygig out of old milk cartons at this time of the day. Some more lights should be on.

Immediately to Leonard's left, through a patch of crowded trees, lay the compound built by Will Daniels. Viewed from Leonard's house, the oblong parking garage for 20 vehicles with a helipad on top cut a silvery grey line across the horizon. From the path he could see the parking garage served as a windscreen for the glass and cedar pyramid, the principal residence.

The edges of the pyramid were chrome steel and the tip had a stained glass lantern lit by a blue propane flame. The reflection of the flame on the steel seemed to lift the building in the air. Suspension of belief came to mind. To the side was the Buckminster Fuller-inspired dome, like a giant lost golf ball tucked in the woods. Built as a greenhouse/powerplant the dome was framed in wrought iron, and during the day the triangles folded out, their solar panel undersides soaking up energy to store in batteries in the garage.

Will Daniels was off the grid. He had his own grid. He had his own micro hydro plant built over the brook flowing down his property. He told Leonard if he had the wires and pipes laid he would let him hook into the arrangement of lights and underground heated

187

glycol he was installing in his part of the lane leading to their properties. Will told Leonard he would take care of the shared entrance before the lane split anyways, and actually sought his permission.

Ed came over a few times to watch the contractors lay the pipes to heat the common driveway. He was in total awe.

"Buddy has no problem with power," Ed said. One of the workmen told him the garage was painted with a special solar collection material made in a Chinese nanotechnology lab for that Korean company, the big one that went bankrupt, the one the teachers lost all that pension money on. All the African miners for the key rare metals keeled over and died, their skeletons dissolved by the substance. Ed saw video from a Belgian crew of the last miners spitting up gelatinous blood as their bones turned to dust.

The compound was not visible from any of the earth view services on the internet. Neither was Antitocia, Leonard's spa here in Logy Bay. Leonard made inquiries. All they could tell him was the overhead photos of that side of the bay were the ones given to them, and they were not expecting any updates. Leonard's lane, the one he shared with Will Daniels, was not on the car navigation systems either. This could have caused a lot of grief for his guests, but they treated the inconvenience as part of the appeal, the allure of really being off the grid of public surveillance, with cappuccinos and blueberry tarts.

This part of the path was not on the maps published by those trail buggers either. This was Leonard's place.

Ed showed Leonard a satellite photo he managed to get from one of his contacts. The rectangle garage was based on the golden mean. The pyramid's base was a part of this progression, and the dome's diameter fit the scale as well. It looked like a kid spilled his designer toys on the side of the hill.

Leonard could easily imagine none of this being here, like the public electronic view. He could see Amherst eyeing these shores in 1762 from his war vessel, looking for a place to make land, to rout the French. He knew there was little record that he and his son were on this rabbit run with a dozen Germans in between, on their way to have a small campfire. He was fine with all this, his personal browsing experience.

The Germans were in awe of Will's fiery fountain, and repulsed - perhaps due to the whole 'water' kick they were all on, Leonard figured. Bud signalled to the group to keep moving, and to be quiet, as Daniels did not know about this trail on the edge of his property.

They passed down the path a short distance, and went between two massive outcrops. Everyone was told to kill the lights as they passed through the rocks, and to be extra careful. Being on the edge of geography has its own special vertigo, one you can never shake. Be here long enough and it becomes a reliable gyro.

From this crook the view offered no sign of land besides the rockface to the right. There was only ocean, and the sound of scree becoming beach below. The moon was visible near the horizon. Soon it would be behind the side-curtain of cliff, creating cross lighting, painting the scene blue black with choruses of wind. The air was new.

The third German tripped and fell. The others froze, paper cutouts against the white waning moon.

"My jeesly head. Who kicked me in my jeesly head!" said Ed Kelly. He was sitting up, flaying his arms. Leonard could see Ed was naked, and the there was a good chance at least one of the Germans had shit themselves, according to the smell.

"Another week of leakage," Leonard thought to himself. *Two weeks of leakage,"* once he remembered accurately the length of the Germans stay.

At least they found Ed. It seemed like Bud's stoking the sauna with fir and kush pellets had the desired effect on Ed, and then some. The Germans would be very relaxed starting on the morrow.

Light from the moon, refracted through the lens of a cloud, flooded the ocean below.

"Light up the fire, Daxen. Let's enjoy the night," Leonard said. He threw Ed a blanket. "I have something that will take care of that pain in yer head, Ed b'y. You pain in the arse."

Ed laughed.

'Come to the Edge of the World' the ads said. The Germans wouldn't forget this as long as they lived. It might be the last structured memory they have of this visit in years to come, if things work out. After this outing, the Germans were going in for saunas, like Ed had, before he disappeared.

Bud moved so Daxen could easily find the wood for the fire. The others eagerly pitched in. Leonard gave them a box of strike matches and a small cloth soaked in lighter fluid he had tied on his walking stick.

Bud gave everyone a cup of Leonard's homemade cider - Aqua Vitae. Daxen lit the fire.

He said "The brain is mostly Water you know Mr Livingstone. I cannot wait until my brain is mostly Newfoundland water."

Leonard raised his mug in a toast.

"We're surrounded by the Amniotic Ocean," Ed said. "May we always stay young, stay true, and stay wet!"

Everyone drank. Leonard loved his job. He loved the view.

Seg 6703 imprint, DNA fragment, Avalon Wilderness

Hiding

MICHELLE ENTERED Leonard's bedroom carrying a large bag. She threw it on Leonard's king size bed, and a terry cotton bathrobe spilled out.

The room was massive. It went from the front of the house back to the driveway. In a renovation overlooked by Diane, Leonard had joined two rooms to make this space. Two 'gunslot' windows were on the long wall. The end of the room facing the ocean was all glass, floor to ceiling, side to side. In the middle of the room, along the walls, there were two blocks that went all the way to the 15' low arched roof. In the middle of the ceiling there was a massive skylight the same proportions as the end window.

In the right spot, on the bed, the effect of the two blocks along the side made the space seem like a large lens, a camera to the infinite world. All you could see through the windows from this position was the ocean and the sky. You felt like you were looking at forever.

When it was stormy the view made you want to pray.

Michelle went to the small block on the western wall and drew back the heavy curtain. There was a small toilet. The interior was tiled in green-black elongated diamond shapes. The walls went right up to the ceiling. Halfway up there was a square window/vent that spilled light inside the enclosure. If you like shitting while sitting in a hole it was a good effect.

Between the two central blocks was a strip of grass, across the middle of the two joined rooms.

She walked across the grass to the other larger, block. The space had an arch in the roomside wall, which continued up to the ceiling. Here was a large tiled tub, crystal white. The faucet was in the wall. She leaned over and started a bath.

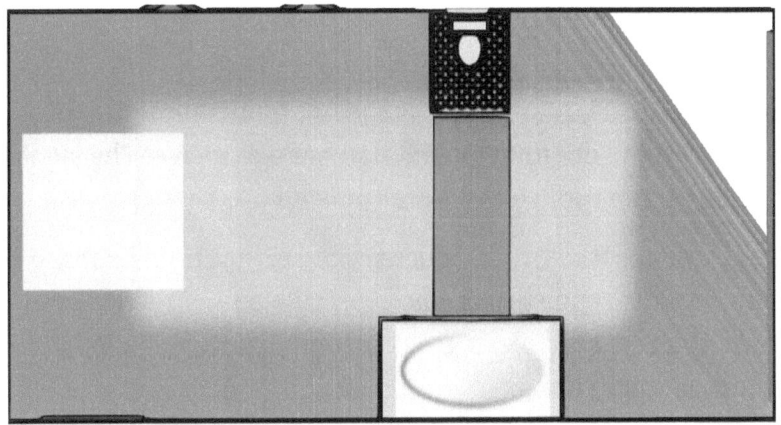

Leonard's Bedroom – AutoDescript Chamber

Michelle needed a break.

She had cleaned up the kitchen after everyone left to go up to the lookout. Then she made the beds and left the note reminding the guests they were expected to take care of the beds etc. during their stay. Colleen went up the road to see her aunt.

Finally some peace and quiet.

She took off her clothes and laid them on the edge of the bed. She emptied the bag, and carried her bathrobe and two towels to the bathtub. She took a small joint out of a pocket in the bathrobe and turned on the music system, picking a blues channel. She enjoyed the blues more after she worked hard.

She went to a small fridge in the adjoining part and retrieved a soft drink.

She sat on the tub and lit the joint. She had the fan turned on and the smoke scooped out a vent, high in the wall.

Michelle stepped in the tub. She pulled a knob and the water stopped falling out of the faucet. In a second it started to rain at the far end of the tub. There was a curtain of water falling from grooves high on the wall.

The four walls formed a column of space above the tub, capped by a clear skylight. The skylight was the full footprint of the tub. From the tub the opening looked flat, but expansive. The skylight was tilted on the roof so the water poured off.

Michelle had a bath here in February once, that time Leonard had gone to Toronto, and she watched the steam melt the ice on the skylight. It all seemed like a great accomplishment, burning the weather just by bathing.

At the armrest level the walls were smooth. At standing waist level there were two bands of bluegrass embedded into the walls. Shafts of two oars acted as handles at the rain end of the enclosure.

Michelle looked up to the sky through the falling water. Her fingers rested on the sidewalls, tickled by the grass. She looked down at the water splashing around her. The reflection of the stars danced around her knees. She felt weightless, tethered to the world by the mere touch of her fingers.

She washed her hair and soaped her body. Then she sat in the tub and let the warm water fall and wash the soap off.

She listened to fourteen songs, making the small room rain when she figured it helped the music.

Michelle pulled the plug and reached for the oar-handles. She lifted herself and twisted. The handles held fast, but one moved about two inches, and the other vectored opposite. With this the back portion of the wall, below the grass and above the bottom shelf, moved sideways about half an inch. She put her fingers in the crack and slid the wall completely away, it was countersunk into the structure and must have been on rails.

Here were three bags, old Crown Royal velvet bags. Michelle picked one up and pulled out a heavy jewel encrusted cross.

This was perfect. She needed a place to hide a few jewels herself. Just perfect.

Image from Don's tablet, Binary Recovery Unit – Fogo Facility

Secrets

Michelle has a discussion with Leonard outside the house, near a root cellar, near some bushes.

If I told you, I'd be putting your life in danger. More danger than you realize.

I'm okay with that.

Let me decide that.

I plan to put your life in danger.

No thank you.

And I'd like you to return the favour.

Absolutely not.

Your story is about those jewels.

Perhaps.

My story is about jewels as well. Other jewels.

I don't want to hear about it.

I want to tell you.

Why.

I need to tell someone. In case something happens.

I'm okay not knowing. Especially if you expect me to tell.

Does anyone else know your story?

No.

We have more in common.

196

Leonard relaxed.

I'm just going to tell you. I have jewels, jewels that have been passed down to me that are worth quite a bit of money. But they are worth more than that, because they are an answer to a dream.

Leonard listened.

They are from the treasure of Coco Island, the treasure that 'Treasure Island' was all about. There's a silver platter with the map to the treasure etched on the back.

Is that it?

Yes.

A treasure map.

Fine. You don't want to know the story behind what I have. How did you find them anyway?

I slipped, in the bath. I told you.

You are welcome to hide your treasure jewels in the stash. You don't need to know what I have. It's a curse, best hidden in the dark.

I'm fine with that.

I'll take pictures. Encrypt them and give them to Bud. In case something happens to me, he will know.

Cool.

MindShare

At night. Leonard and Ludwig are on the back deck. They have a drink of cider.

You can say we are fortunate Leonard. May I call you Leonard?

Certainly. Call me Len, Ludwig.

We are doing what we want to do. We are water people. Most of us grew up on rivers or lakes. And we remember them being pure. And we realize it makes you a different person, being around good fine water.

I remember being in Toronto. I was thinking of moving there. And my friend, Tim, went out one day to get some groceries. I asked him what he was getting, and his listed off many items. But then he said water. It was the first time I ever heard of anyone saying they were buying water.

We are all buying water now Len.

I guess. I guess I don't know any different.

You never moved there, to Toronto?

No. I figured if they had me buying water I'd do just about anything to be there. Didn't want to whore myself out.

Good decision. You do not know what is in city water. Trace drugs, estrogen, heavy metals, all attack your immune system. Moving water, river water, should be clean water.

So, are you a river person?

Yes. My grandfather had a watermill. Outside Mainz. It had been in the family for six generations. Owners of such industries change with the powers that be, generally.

I grew up with the sound of water. The taste in the air, the smell all around. Fields and trees soaked in water. The river the watermill was on would rise every year, four meters, and it would leave all kinds of things when it shrank. More and more non-degradable debris would be left behind. I remember the smell mostly. The smell of decay is sweet. The smell of useless trash is sharp. Unpleasant.

Plenty of that around here. People dump shit everywhere.

The ocean is different altogether than streams and rivers. It is the bank of life. Its size is unknowable. Creatures live there we don't even know about. They've been there since the sun turned on.

The water you are drinking is older than the sun.

So you guys make any money at this? Or are you all rich?

Some of us don't have to work. Three are invited guests, and as such they pay for three of the group. Daxen has sixteen million followers on social media. I have a blog, write for several online publications and have six ebooks. We do okay.

We all worked in publishing. That world is gone.

Publishing anything must be a bitch nowadays.

It is. Books are for purists. But the market is growing, in electronic media, especially in South Asia.

People still hungry for the words of the colonizers.

Well, their local governments are corrupt as you can get. Europe has had a lot of conflict, but in South Asia they have been fighting with each other since the dawn of time.

Mindshare must be a different game down there. Probably in Europe as well.

How do you mean?

When I was young there were only a handful of television stations. Enough books for you to read to get a good understanding of things, and you had your pick of great music.

We all drank from the same well, so to speak, of a common culture. And as such we all sort of thought of the same thing. The Russians were our enemies. We weren't too fond of you guys, that mess you were in the middle of. And there were lots of great movies.

And we knew then. We knew that everything could go to shit. One of the first things they figured out with all the computers and such was how much of everything there was, and how much we had left. It didn't look good.

And we all shared many of these thoughts. We knew what to do, what to fix. It was all doable. Then everything broke loose. Multi-media.

Now everything is fragmented. There is no shared experience. Or there are too many.

So there's no common ground. Junk has been dumped in our public spaces.

Social media is mindshare. It is public. It is nasty.

I do not have much to do with that. High school pics, and all.

Much different in Europe Mr Livingstone. Much different.

There is a great thirst for our musings Len, especially in South Asia. For many people arguing the environment argument is their best hope for real change.

Daxen has many followers, and our website, well the servers are at capacity. But this distribution can easily be shut down. And we really have to fight now to keep the network accessible.

A man in Uruguay has assembled Daxen's tweets into a core part of environmental preachings, which have taken off in Indonesia. They have a church where they read out one of his aphorisms as a group. The videos, well they are mesmerizing. To think something that may have been posted two days ago could make it into a religious ceremony today, in a closed down warehouse in Jakarta, or in field on the coast of Malaysia, is something we have to live with.

So my feeling of mindshare is quite different. It is science non-fiction, and communication fact.

No shit. Wild.

From canine pen, Avalon Wilderness

E D MOVED HIS NECK to make a gap in the seal of the sauna. A sprout of steam streamlined over his jawline. He laughed.

Earlier, Ed watched the saunas get hooked up, and Bud said he was welcome to be the first to try one of them out.

Bud put some sawdust in the hopper and started the box for Ed. He opened the two doors at the front, each with a large Bakelite knob dead center. One adjusted heat and the other the humidity. Small knobs on the inside had access to the same adjustments.

After Ed was seated, with his head positioned in the cut-out for the neck, Bud closed the slanting front doors.

"Good for ya!" Bud said, sealing the steel box. "See you later."

Ed was in the steam box for over an hour. He had fallen asleep, a few times. Deeper and deeper each time.

Ed pushed the doors open and steam rushed out. In a beat his body started to cool down, releasing blood into his head, He fainted. For a minute. He woke. His head felt like it was detached from his body. There was a slight buzz in his ear.

He barely had a dial tone.

He got up and made for the spring, up the hill. Diane said in the life of water, the spring was where water was born. He wondered if he could baptize himself.

Doda

LEONARD'S GRANDMOTHER leaned over the kitchen table and lifted the window sash, tapping it upward with the butt of her hand.

"Put in the screen now Len, while I holds 'er up."

The screen was a wooden machine, a window on its side Leonard figured, with a fixed height and its own sash design to adjust to the width of the window. Leonard put the screen in the window well and adjusted it tight.

A melody of smells flooded into the kitchen. Freshly cut hay was the main note, with a tinch of freshly turned earth from the garden. Some gasoline from the motor Pop had been working on in the shed, wood drying and wood rotting released complimentary chords. A distant brush fire from a few fields over was evident.

Workshirts and pants were in full sail on the clothesline.

The smell of the sea was mixed with the items that bore it - the fishing net being repaired in the yard, Pop's boots and socks in the porch, the fur of the large dog, Blackie, lying in the shade of the shed at the back of the house.

Blackie was an outport variety dog. He was one of several dogs named 'Blackie' in the area. He didn't so much as have an owner, as a person or group of people he choose to spend his time with. At times he was referred to as 'Old Blackie'. A derivative of the mastiff St. John's breed, Blackie was a water dog who liked to work. He hauls nets in the summer and wood in the winter, retrieves buoys on the water and served as lifeguard on Pop's small inshore dory.

Nan helped Leonard make the screen steadfast and opened the door to the porch as well as the two doors on the back, the main door and the storm door.

"That will help with the air flow," she said. "Hungry Len?"

Leonard shook his head. He looked down at the yellow dumptruck he kept as a toy at his grandparent's house. There were about 20 carpenters in the bed of the truck, Leonard's playful pickings for the morning.

"Toss them outside Leonard. Them gives me the creeps," Nan said.

Leonard picked up the dumptruck and walked out on the step to the porch. He backed it up to the edge and lifted the lever releasing the bed of the truck so he could dump the insects out. He had to shake the truck so they all fell into the long grass at the base of the back steps.

The porch was in the shade from the front of the house. The fields beyond were alight with golden tips of long stalks of grass Pop was getting ready to cut for animal feed and bedding.

A small white butterfly angled across the tops of the grass. A large cat's paw, at the end of a slender barn cat, batted the butterfly out of the air. Leonard could see some of the tips of grass move more than the others.

"Harvey caught a butterfly!" he said re-entering the kitchen.

"Poor Harvey" Nan said, flattening the oilcloth on the kitchen table with her strong hands.

She looked Leonard in the eye, and her face went full glint.

"Yesterday, when I was in the rocking chair, rocking, I rocked over Harvey's tail," she said.

"What did he say?" Leonard asked, enjoying the routine.

"It won't be long now," Nan answered.

They both laughed.

Nan had a proud kitchen. It looked clean. It smelled clean. It felt comfortable. There was a side with a sink and the cupboard for most of the dishes. On the other side there was a long countertop with cupboards for food. A tin breadbox was in the corner at one end of the counter, on the other end there was a toaster and a small transistor radio. The bottom cupboard, behind the door to the hallway, was where the 'working' liquor was kept - rums and whiskies for droppers-by.

In between was the stove, a unit with an oil side and a wood side, with a small oven. Against the outside wall was the window and the kitchen table, used for meals and cards.

On one end of the kitchen was a small room, big enough for a daybed, a small table with the television on it, and a telephone table. Beneath a small shelf for the shortwave was a large wooden box full of records with a record player on top. A pantry under the stairs hid behind a curtain of beads and lengths of weighted cloth.

The small fridge was in the space underneath the stairs. Leonard knew Nan hid chocolate in there, and Pop had a flask of dark navy rum, in an old burlap bag from India, beneath the crib board. Leonard liked to hide in the back of the space, and Nan would stomp on the stairs above his head yelling his name, never with a hint of fear.

At the other end of the kitchen was the door to the inside porch. There was a small window and a long rough counter against the outside wall. It had a large bin for wood accessed by lifting a lid built in the countertop. The cold cupboard for food was on one end of the outer wall, on the other end a variety of tools was neatly hung, just inside the door. The outside doors - a solid door with a deadbolt, and an outside pine door closed with a latch – were at the end of the inner hallway.

A newspaper was spread out on the counter of the inside porch. On it were collections of plants and flowers: Dandelions, St. John's wort, poppy flowers, and paper bags with mushrooms and lichen. Leonard had spent the afternoon watching his grandmother take from this counter and boil or steam the plants in iron pots on the stove. The heat and the smell was why they had to open the window and make way to the door.

"Watcha makin?" Leonard asked.

"Some tea. Special tea. For Pop and the men who will be cutting the hay."

Leonard loved the cutting of the hay. It was his favourite time of the year. Enough people would show up to get all the hay cut on the land in one day. Some would come by for the whole day, Pop's brothers and nephews, some would come by for the afternoon or early late summer evening. It was better than a country fair. There were no strangers.

And there'd always be the crowd of distant cousin kids; the older ones trying to get the younger ones to help build the massive piles of hay collected in the fields. The younger ones made a show of helping, but when they figured the time was right, or the haystack was big enough, they would climb on top and have a game of King of the Castle, trying to push one another off the top.

Some girls played the gentler games, when they happened, or showed the youngest how to braid ropes of grass, or how to chase butterflies in the funnest way possible. Some were rough.

Nan handed a roll of aluminium foil to Leonard and instructed him to tear off two pieces about 8 inches long.

She laid the first piece of foil on the oilcloth and covered it in red flower petals. She laid the second piece of foil over these, with a gap at one end. She laid some plants on this foil. Leonard jumped back a little when he saw the giant stingernettle stack amongst the plant matter. It wasn't the size of the stalk that surprised him, rather it was the realization that it had been handled and cut into sections. Stingernettles - ouch.

Nan took the rolling pin and squeezed the water out of the plant stalks, pushing it onto the petals. She added a few more drops of water, some mushrooms, some of the St. John's wort, and then folded up the foil in a packet. She tilted back the lid of the stove and placed the foil package into the fire of the stove, catching a corner of it as the lid was returned so the packet was suspended in the flame of the stove's fire.

"Your great-great- grandfather learned how to make this tea in India. He brought the seeds from Persia, that's why we call it *Persian* tea. They call it *doda*," she said as she cleared off the table.

She grabbed the stove-lid handle and levered it into the lid. "I makes my own kind. Making it is even better than drinking it. Ready to take a deep breath, Leonard."

She trapped the corner of the foil sticking out with a fork against the stovetop and slid the lid off. With another fork she flipped the foil package out of the fire onto the lid. With the two forks she poked holes in the foil.

She leaned over the foil. "Ready Len!" she smiled. She pulled two large beach rocks out of her apron and scrunched them down on the foil, releasing a thick blue smoke that seemed to stick to her hair, and then disappear up her nostrils or down her mouth. Leonard mimicked her, pouncing on imaginary smoke. His hands squeezed on a pulp paperback of Treasure Island.

She grabbed the foil between the two rocks and dropped it all in the pot stewing on the stove, the rocks trapping the foil to the bottom of the pot.

"Put on a Johnny Cash record Leonard, and we has a snuggle on the daybed. Nan needs a catnap," she said, removing her apron.

Leonard placed the disk on the turntable and dropped the needle. He adjusted the volume as the music owned the rooms.

"I meant the other side, you dodo," she laughed. "That's okay." She sat behind Leonard on the daybed.

"I'm not a dodo. Dodos are extinct. There's no more Dodos."

"I'll tell you what's extinct. Great Auks are extinct. The last one was seen in Newfoundland. Did you know that?" Leonard shook his head.

"There were the penguins of the North Atlantic. Penguin is the ancient name for Great Auks. When they saw birds on the ice in Antarctica they called them penguins, because they thought they were Great Auks. Did you know that?"

"No. How do you know so much Nan? You knows way more than Mom. Probably more than Dad even."

Nan laughed. "I reads a lot, Leonard. Gets you through the winter. Can't travel to Florida like Mr Munroe or Miss Parker, but I can take a cruise with Pirates through the Caribbean right here on this daybed with a good book. And a cup of tea."

Leonard snuck into the pantry and came out with two hard candy. He handed the yellow one to his grandmother.

"I used to be a teacher you know. I had to give it up when I married your Pop. No work for married women in them days." She popped the candy in her mouth.

She lay on the cool daybed with Leonard snuggled into her. She tapped the music on Leonard's elbow and hummed along to the music. When he was asleep she crooked the hard candy out of his mouth with her finger and popped it into her mouth. In another tale of heartbreak she was asleep herself.

She dreamed she was in the boat with Pop and Blackie, past the edge of the cove. The sea was calm. It was foggy and windy, with sheets of ice pellets falling through bursts of light. They came upon an island, a single shaft of rock like the Pillar of Alexander in St. Petersburg. On top of the pillar was a penguin, a sole penguin, last beacon of its kind, squawking into the mist. Nan started to weep and the fog returned, the sound of the penguin fading to nothing.

Leonard knows she had this dream because he had the same one.

Standard background signal

Defining Moments – Colleen

Postcard From Marble Mountain

Hi LizBeth,

I think my career in broadcasting is finished.

At Marble. Was invited along by a crowd I hardly knows. One of them works at the TV station where I filled in few weeks ago. Arrived early. Wanted to make a good impression and needed some practice.

I'm not good with the chair, and I wanted to try some turns in the new gear.

Made it on the chair okay, not too shaky. Had to hurry, bunch of high school girls were lined up behind me.

Got off the chair and had to pee real bad. So I went 'off-piste' (that's ski talk for off the trail) and found a hidden spot where I could relieve myself.

Ripped down my good snowpants (you should see 'em Beth - Pikachu!) and squat. Soon as I started to go I leaned a bit and then the skis started skiing. I couldn't stand up, the pants were around my calfs, and before I knew it I had shot out on the main ski run like a rocket. All the high school girls were there taking selfies. Now videos of me peeing down Marble are all over the internet.

"Gnarly Girl" I think it's called. Can I stay at your place and hide for a while?

Cheers - Colleen

From Jean's camera - Livingstone Homestead

Speed

[Tangential to the core group, these snippets provide context for
pre-events.]

Youth

J EAN HAS THE FRESHNESS OF YOUTH adults appreciate. Her beautiful smile, her bright eyes and the way she looks slightly above the horizon is a force of hope. She looks to a future many older people will not live to see. By being among older people, Jean makes them feel safe, optimistic.

Her brief installation piece was a big hit. She set up a potter's bench in a small downtown gallery and built vertical gardens with the members of the audience. She was miked and the conversations she had with the guests were delivered through 12 speakers in the rooms. It took her three days, and by the end of the second day there were line-ups down the block to get in during the performance.

There have been some offers for her to do it again as a fundraiser. Cancers, Diseases, Mental Health, Children in Crisis, and Women in Need - you name it. She is almost afraid to pick one, because others would be okay with being the second or third event, the fourth or the fifth even.

Colleen said she might have something special Jean could do for ten weeks and get paid, well. And Colleen picked the coffee shop, a new spot for Jean.

Colleen was there, hopeful, in a skirt. The weather called for chances of sun, and she was inviting it out.

"Jean, good to see you again."

Their families shared some of the same circles when Jean was in her early teens, and Colleen, though a bit older, liked to hang out with Jean. Colleen has been back downtown a lot lately, and they bump into each other on Water and Duckworth streets.

"I like this place. It's comfy."

"Best 5 bean salad this side of Jobs Cove."

"Well, sounds good."

"Check the menu. It's gold."

The waitress came by to take their order.

Jean went with the mooseburger, offering a small apology. "I need the protein. I can feel it."

"Great. I'm having the lamb stew."

"There are ways we can hire you for the whole summer, ten weeks. The issue is how much do we want to make."

"Sounds good."

"We would like you to do an installation at an old folk's home. Some of these have 200-300 residents. You can pick one, or do a few at the same time. It depends how big you want to go with it."

"In an old folks home. Interesting. How will you pay?"

"We have a few options. If there are ways to get everyone involved, as a performance we can say they are audience members. And we have sponsors who will pay attendance for any seniors to one of our shows. So whatever 'size' show you can do, or how 'many' shows you do, we can figure it out. We just need some reasonable numbers. I'd like to see if there's a way to raise some money for the home, or homes, as well, through a pay event at the end, if possible. We can go above scale. Just tell me what you need."

"Old folk's homes. That would be cool. I like old people. I want to become one someday."

In the next booth, two young Indonesian males sit with a young Chinese male. The Indonesians are wanting to buy some explosives, enough to blow up a car. The Chinese male has the explosives, but he wants them to do him a favour. He doesn't need cash, besides they do not have any. He wants them to mess up the bistro across the street, the one owned by the French Canadians. Stuff insurance won't cover. Then they can blow up some Germans with the explosives.

From plant material - Livingstone Homestead

WITNESSES SAY the middle-aged French woman slumped over and fell on the floor, dead. Then they noticed the snakes on the floor. Two of them. The best Vietnamese noodle restaurant closed down, and one of the French Canadian owners was found dead in his condo later the same day.

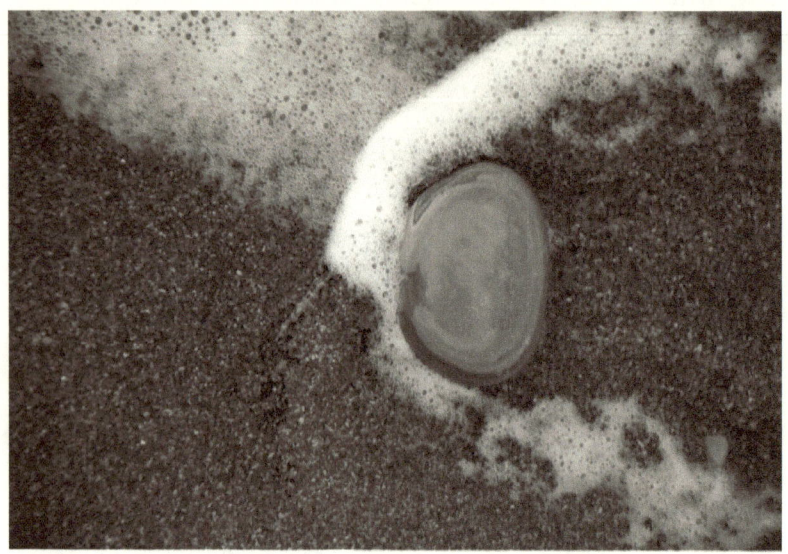

Common signal, defining shorelines

THE ROOM, really half a basketball court, with a net, great floors and a small set of risers against one wall, became quiet. A projection, the words "Operation Killick" shines on the wall opposite. A lot of young men and women are sitting on the risers. Clean cut, mostly.

A military man addresses the group. His name is Captain Alphonse Ledwell.

"Reports have come in on a possible attack on some German tourists staying at a spa in Logy Bay, the Antitocia. There are anywhere from 8 to 12 members in the party, but one guest, a Daxen Friedlander, is the main target. Mr Friedlander is an environmentalist from Germany.

There is chatter that some south Asians may be here trying to assassinate Friedlander, as he is revered in South Asia, specifically Indonesia, by people who are fighting the government in these regions.

This is the first assignment of this joint anti-terrorism unit. You are here from the Royal Newfoundland Constabulary, the Royal Canadian Mounted Police, and Canadian Special Forces. I look forward to success in this mission.

We have some of the 'who' in this situation. We know of some of the 'why', though it is difficult to understand. The 'when' as far as we are concerned is as long as the guests are on Canadian soil. I will hand this over to Sergeant Larwinski from the RCMP to discuss the 'what and how' of this operation, named 'Operation Killick'."

Sergeant Larwinski stepped forward, tapped on the screen and a picture of a pair of nun chucks snapped on the display wall.

217

"South Asian assassins can be silent and deadly, or they make a big bang. They are experts at silent close-in kills – knives, strangulation, and closing the air supply. Their knowledge of explosives and remote technology gives them considerable reach when they cannot get too close to a target. They tend to use firearms amongst themselves. They like to work in groups of two or three.

The slide changed to a clear high definition satellite image of Leonard's property.

"The place where the target is staying is fairly easy to monitor. A large house, up a long lane, off a tertiary road with no other real entry or exit points. Access off the nearby water is doubtful, and easily guarded against. The property is off public satellite data, so anyone wanting preliminary information will have to do so in person.

"The most likely attacks can be in public spaces. If these guests ever leave the spa, any transportation used by the target is closely monitored. Blowing up vehicles is a common pattern, most likely with improvised explosive devices. Attacks in popular public spaces are rare. Parking lots, city parks and remote bus stations are preferred locations for assassinations.

"The first thing we have to do is find our suspects. We have to keep watching and listening."

He taps the screen again, showing a picture of the spa from its website.

"The spa has one week and two week bookings. The German party arrived two days ago. We have been watching the property since yesterday. The locals are aware of our presence, it's hard not to stick out. They think we are a special patrol for Will Daniels, owner of the hockey team. His property is adjacent to the Antitocia Spa. Some other locals expect we are performing surveillance on Ed Kelly, a cantankerous troublemaker who lives in the area as well.

"Our main means of surveillance has been a pair on bicycles, two joggers and a patrol car.

"These individuals, the bikers and the joggers, currently on duty, are all a part of the QComm initiative. Constable Henry Driscoll from the Royal Newfoundland Constabulary, Sergeant June Fenwick with the Royal Canadian Mounted Police, and special Officers John Kelland and Nancy Franchez all have implants which allow them to communicate silently to one another."

Sergeant Larwinski taps the screen, displaying a picture of a head, ¾ view from the rear, with a small square chip with a tiny antennae sticking up behind the subject's ear. A finger is bending the lobe forward to afford a clearer view.

"This technology is able to read their brainwaves, a special part of the brain they have been trained to use – the brain is a muscle, you can train parts of it I'm told – and these messages are broadcast. We have an app on our phones that can pick up these messages. As well, the officers can receive the messages without hand held devices, through the chip behind their ears. It's exciting stuff. Stealth communications"

He swipes across a tablet, "Let's see what they are saying, shall we." A messaging window opens up, pictures of the four faces of the officers along the top.

John Kelland's picture highlights, then the message appears.

"No noodles tonight ducky."

Henry Driscoll's face highlights.

"Dad always would make a joke when we passed that place he said used to be the Moon Palace. Something about flies in fries."

June Fenwick's face highlights.

"I need to pee."

Sergeant Larwinski laughed. Then the room rumbled with polite chuckles.

"This is what they call 'Beta' testing. I'm impressed. Let's catch some bad guys, or easier yet, not give some guys the chance to be bad."

James McLeod
12 hrs · 👥

You start to think about how weird it's gotten when you notice that there are ingredients listed on the side of the Dasani bottle.

From radio signals, reassembled digital telegram

.

THE SILK BAG was once Derek's mother's, a bag for expensive lipstick, a gift from his dad. The silk thread was something he stole when he was just a kid. The rawhide he picked up at a workclothes market in Cakung. The ball bearings, they were from a box of his Dad's possessions. The rock was from a beach near his girlfriend's home.

Interior of a condo near the waterfront, looking out the narrows. Early evening, the sun has capped the Southside Hills opposite. The copper letters of the Atlas Center catch the fading light. The solar panelled roof to the raised rock cork murmur mists of light. Through the glow, the top of a slowly turning vertical turbine can be seen, the structure footed on the Freshwater Bay side of the hill.

We see, in silhouette, a man walk through the frame. A buzzer goes off. The man goes to the intercom, briefly coming into frame. "Who is it?"

"Derek and Remy from Witless Pizza. We heard what happened in your shop today. We're here to do you a solid. We have a medium Settler's Feast, and a large Masterless special."

The man has his face close to the intercom. He is sweating. "Pizza?"

"We figure you've had a hard day, with the snake and all."

"Okay. Come on up." The man presses the button. He walks toward the picture window. The horizon seems tilted. He stamps his foot. He turns and comes back towards the door.

Knock. Luc opens the door. There are two South Asian men. The first one grabs him low around the waist, pinning his arms. The other swings a kind of punch at him. Luc is unconscious and falling to the floor. The first one turns him on his stomach. Luc's legs twitch, a comic attempt to run, or crawl.

In Derek's hand is a rock. It has a hole drilled in it. On the bottom is a large washer, wrapped in silk thread, flush against the surface. The silk thread goes through the rock and braids around the rawhide strings which pass through the fingers of Derek's closed fist. The rawhide is bound together in a rope for about the length of a pop can, then it ends in a sling. The rawhide nests around the silk bag, and inside the bag there are nine ball bearings.

Derek waits for Remy to get up, and listens for anyone in the hallway.

A ship's horn blasts in the harbour. The glass in the window refracts the sound, making it longer than initiated. The natural frequency in the room amplifies the boom with several levels of disturbing harmonics. The ground seems to give way.

Derek swings the lethal ballchuck at the man lying face down on the floor. One more crack at the base of his skull and Luc is good as dead.

IN AN OFFICE under renovation we see a young woman writing on a piece of paper, referencing a screen. She finishes and begins to walk. It is late in downtown Montevideo, Uruguay.

She enters an informal meeting area and sits next to a young man.

"Darius, they have not been to the well today. There are only a few messages. A couple make no sense."

"We will have to do the best we can, with what we have, Krista. We should have enough time."

They review the notes. Darius draws a few lines on the page, writes in the margin. They watch the clock on the wall. As it approaches noon Darius starts to type a message into a phone.

In Indonesia we see a variety of people.

A man in office building. Couple on city park bench. Three purveyors in a local street mart. Four men pushing a tractor down a dirt road. Five abalone farmers on a boat, fixing a wharf. Six woman smashing aluminum cans. A dozen children playing a game in a field. Fifty people gathered in a wooden grove. A hundred people walk along a beach. A thousand people gather outside an office building.

Darius hits send.

Their phones beep. They read the screen, scrolling. They whisper the message after reading it, working their words into one voice, all facing the same direction. The direction is the building, the headquarters of *Holstu-Molloy, Extraction Industries*, Kuala Lumpur.

The man in the office building looks down at the crowd below.

Darius joins his thumbs together, stretches out his arms, and looks through the viewfinder of his hands.

Finished, they speak aloud, in English.

> We all drink from the same well.
>
> Water is life. Life is water.
>
> Destroy water, destroy me.
>
> Water, from the wild, tames us.

The prayer finished hard, strong. The people raise thin glass bottles, a kind of pocket flask, and hold them to their chests. Then, grinning, they say,

> The seventh water will set us free.
>
> (*Laughter*)
>
> Let us drink, while we wait for our release.

The people in Indonesia all sip water from their glass flasks, six deliberate sips. They hold the flask to the sky.

Krista checks her screen.

"We have new orders for 41,388 flasks."

Darius smiles. "I made them laugh today."

The man in the office building taps and types, "News?"

A Tartan of Experiences

[secondary orbits, necessary to keep the system stable.]

Rajith

FIONA PAUSED, letting the fridge door swing.

"We have the same taste buds, you and I. The same cells in the eyeballs that pick up light. Sound bangs the drum in my ear just like it does yours. But the difference is in the mind, how we register those experiences. In my mind, and in all women's minds, there are threads of connections, each with the perception of time as a common strand. When we taste, our brain sparks the information into the fire of our soul, where it lives with all these other ghosts of past experiences. We just don't taste 'salt' – we taste change, the story of the people who made the salt, who sold it, how happy their children are.

"Sometimes I think all men taste is melting rocks.

"Our mind sees the sun rise and fall just once. Our soul is the belief it can happen again. Our emotions want to bring these two together, mind and soul, with the knowledge they are never in the same room. Our experiences weave this tartan of the mind and soul around the whole lot to find the peace. Peace is the harmony, where one sensation flows into the next, and will continue. We need to know, as sure as the sun sets, it also rises. Tears are a sign we are trying. We try."

Rajith adjusted the bags of groceries on the kitchen counter. "You're really upset," he said.

Fiona glared at him. She made a show of dropping a head of lettuce into the garbage bucket at her feet.

Rajith thought he saw gills, flaring.

225

She wiped a tear with a tissue, drawn from the *Oak Valley Memories – Kitchen Box*.

"Yes, I'm upset."

"All I said was I did not know if you liked shopping for food more than you like throwing it out. That's all."

"They're past their time Raj. This smells. Leftovers never get eaten. You have some food projects in here that have to go."

"Okay. I didn't know it was upsetting your soul."

"There's a lot of things you don't know, Rajith. Don't underestimate what you don't know."

Fiona took out a low walled glass container with some plastic wrap limply serving as a lid.

Rajith stirred. "Am I being bullied? Over a head of lettuce. And some Cajun Butter Chicken, which you said you liked."

Fiona glared. "I said that two weeks ago. Now it's Cajun *Why The Fuck Are You Still In The Fridge* Butter Chicken."

"We eat out too much," Rajith said, removing a frozen packet of South American fish from a bag.

"I can't stand to open this fridge."

"Why don't you do something else, and I'll take care of this."

"Good idea." Fiona moved the bucket back along the floor and closed the fridge. She laid the food container on the counter, forcing a space for it amongst the unbagged groceries.

As she left the kitchen Rajith stared into space and said "I hope this is not a trick."

Fiona stopped in the hallway. "You're asking for it mister."

"I mean, there's a lot I don't know that's good. Right?" he said. "There's a lot of good about you, about being with you, that I can't share, I can't explain. You feel the same, right."

"Clean the fridge. That will be good."

Rajith opened a package of jellied cookies. "Precious," he mouthed.

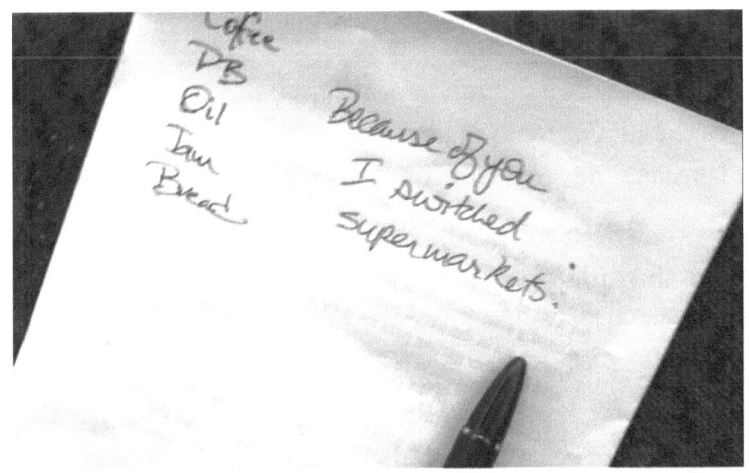

Luke's phone

Billy

THE MORNING SUN HAD RISEN over the hills of the harbour and the rise of the old city and was peeking down into the Rennies Mill valley. The light flooded Billy Young's room, waking him with its creeping heat. He glared through the wall to ceiling window, through his back yard, awash in a fog of light, to the backyards of the houses opposite, still in shadow – silhouettes behind a radiant curtain.

First light was Billy's favourite part of the day, though he rarely saw it as the primary act in his cycle. A regular part of his pattern is to witnesses the sun rising as his eyes shutter close for the day.

His life was against the grain of most people, which suited him fine. More the flip side, the side rarely seen, than the same side as others.

It was a late night. The *Trouble in the Colonies* show had evening performances two nights in a row, one night in Placentia, and he found it difficult to relax, to come down, after. So he'd sleep late, get some stuff done, have a nap, and get ready for the show. Midnight he was wide awake.

He was working most of the night on life-size cameos, in clay, of his parents and his brother Ben. His father's profile sits on a worktable, he had made, along the west wall of the studio room. The table is slanted, like monk's work bench from a scriptoria. It's been a long time. His family have changed, and he does not know how. All he can do is immortalize them.

If anyone asks about the subjects in the pieces he'll say it is just a random study.

His days are free now, at least for a week. The *'Trouble'* show shut down yesterday. Fiona and Tony quit. No replacements. And he was offered a job with the downtown group, they just started something new. They wanted him to help an artist with a project involving plants, starting next week.

He had gone to the auditions for *Trouble in the Colonies* out of a passing interest to see if acting was so hard. A summer working outside would be fun. He might meet some new people.

The director was a bit uptight, and the crowd in the room didn't fit – it didn't seem there was any way this collection of people could publicly do something others would want to see. It was uncomfortable. He felt embarrassed for everyone. Then the director started reading the script. Billy felt like he was in grade two, for the slower group, when schools worked that way.

For some reason he decided to act retarded. It gave him a relaxed distance from the group, but they also found it quite endearing. Acting retarded is what lead him to Newfoundland in the first place, many years ago.

So he got a part on the stupid little play, and had to carry through with the retarded thing for two whole months. That was acting.

It was tough. Several of his neighbours on the Pine Bud had gone to the show. He didn't want to be recognized. So he kept his distance, and left late after the show wrapped.

He was going to have to turn down the art gig. He didn't want to do retarded any more.

Years ago, on a school ski trip to Big White, in British Columbia, he made fun of some Arab guy, trying to rile him up. The kid had a bit of a slur in his speech, and English was a foreign tongue. Billy started making faces, called the guy a retard.

The Arab kid was there with his family. They were looking at buying the ski hill in the Okanagan.

The kid challenged Billy on the hill, bumping him, spraying him. Billy led him into the trees. The kid fell through a sinkhole, banged his head against the tree and died. His father, some sultan, vowed he would have Billy killed, for he had killed a prince, his oldest son.

The prince was the start of the story as how he ended up in St. John's. The princess was the last installment, before he had to go into hiding for good. The Malaysian princess.

Now, there was no way he could go back to Bermuda. Ever.

He still wonders if the attempt on his life was bono fide. The bullets missed him by three feet. And who tries to gun someone down on St. Lawrence market? His life was not his own ever since that 'bang, bang' and the exploding watermelons.

Billy was going to St. Andrew's College, in Aurora, Ontario, Canada. It is an international private school, very popular amongst the families of diplomatic mandarins and business tycoons in the Commonwealth. His dad and his uncle went there. His uncle became a diplomat, an advisor for the banking industry in Bermuda. His uncle had a place in Toronto, worked in the office tower with gold in the windows, and Billy visited him often.

His family had been in banking out of Bermuda since the early 1700's. Starting out they managed the finances for the provisioning of the Scottish settlements in Panama.

The first time Billy saw a secret service agent, or at least the front line administrative branch of the secret services, was after the threat from the Saudi prince.

The death of the young prince turned out to be a huge international issue in Canada. The senior Saudi prince was a significant investor in the Alberta tar sands projects, and after his son died he divested all his interests in Canada.

At first, Billy thought the agents of the Western branch of Canadian Intelligence were there to protect him from the prince.

At the College, two of the teachers were agents, and he had to report to one of them every day, under the cover of tutorials and guidance counselling. Outside of school, such as his frequent trips to the city, there was always an agent within half a kilometer he was told.

They installed an app on his phone. All he had to do was dial #007 and he could see where agents were located. He tried it several times. In school he always knew where Ms. Wiggenshire and Mr Pulua were. In Toronto, there were always at least two red dots on the screen, a block or two away.

The weekend of the shooting Billy was going to fly back to Bermuda with his uncle on his uncle's private jet. They did this about once a month.

He was asked to take packages with him to Bermuda, to do some drops, as a way of gaining trust within the service. Ms. Wiggenshire, his guidance counsellor, said it was a way to draw out if the Saudis were still after him, and his family. She couldn't share the details on who was picking up the packages, or what was in the sealed cases, but she was told from higher ups it would serve as a test to see if anyone was on his trail. He thought it was odd. When your guidance counsellor gives you a study assignment doing espionage, it is pretty exciting for a 16 year old.

He had made four such deliveries. He was picking up the fifth from a cheese vendor at St. Lawrence market when a man approached him, yelled his name and pulled out a gun. He was only seven or eight feet away. The man fired two shots and ran through the crowd out of sight. He missed, and the market was splattered with exploded watermelons

Billy dialled #007 and saw a red dot move away from him, in the same direction as the shooter. It went to Lower Jarvis where it joined another red dot. The two red dots moved north for a couple of blocks. One turned off, then the other. As quick as that two more dots appeared on the screen, one in the market – the cheese vendor - and another approaching.

Billy looked up and saw a young man taking video of him with this phone. He grabbed the phone and ran out of the market. People were still screaming. He started up for St James Park. He dropped both phones on the back bumper of a car stopped in traffic, and then headed back towards the ferry to Toronto Island.

He had a sense the secret service was not there to protect him from the Saudis.

Two agents were there when he approached his uncle's condo. They asked him where the package was, and his phone. He said he was mugged outside the market, and he needed to clear his head. One agent gave him another phone, and another package.

He knew what was in the package. A cd case with a flash disk inside. The flash disk had spreadsheets. They showed all the holdings of all the industries associated with the tar sands – oil companies, suppliers, even environmental groups. The holdings of the Saudi companies were in red, the holdings of a particular Malaysian company were in green. The last spreadsheet had a list of recommended buy and sell options. The spreadsheet was a blueprint for this Malaysian company, *Holstu-Molloy, Extraction Industries*, to strategically take over the claim in the oil sands by the Saudis.

There was more. A similar set was there for the aerospace industry, the forestry sector, and fast food businesses. All prepared for other Malaysian investment firms. He has just saved it to a cloud service when the proprietor of the cybercafé came over and ripped the flash stick out of the computer, claiming it had a virus and was infecting his network, and might put him out of business. The proprietor cursed at Billy in sailor's Tagalog.

After he made the drop in Bermuda his phone buzzed, indicating a time and place for him to pick up a call at the public telephone. On the phone he was told it was not safe for him to return to Canada, and arrangements had been made for him to go to Kuala Lumpur.

There he met a princess, a daughter of one of the seven kings. They fell in love. Then he was told he had to go into hiding. The Malaysians and the Saudis both wanted a part of him. So the Canadian Secret Service set him up in the safest place they knew, in St. John's Newfoundland, in a neighbourhood of academics and cultural mandarins. He could disappear.

But he could never return to Bermuda. Never see his family again.

His family had been told Billy went missing in Hong Kong. They were told Billy had a large gambling debt. He had taken off to Malaysia and Hong Kong on a gambling spree, and it was likely his luck had run out. His father doubted the story, telling his uncle Billy wasn't a kid who took risks. Bankers do not gamble.

Billy is not quite sure he loved the princess, or if she loved him. It was an intense young fling. It was all so unreal. Running away, speed boats to hidden islands, opium in gold pipes, menageries, making love on tiger furs – being watched by a real tiger, caged and growling at the scent - a tortoise shell full of pearls, rain, rain so hard it should have killed everything, colours, real eunuchs, a Malaysian palace guard, a hood over his head, interrogation, and prison – a real dungeon. Rats. Insects. Men with no teeth. An explosion. Men with night goggles. Another hood over his head. Another speedboat. A long flight. Panama. Newfoundland. New papers. New identity. A portfolio of stocks giving him a healthy monthly stipend.

Billy kicked the helmet off the day bed and rolled over. More sleep. The sun warmed the back of his head.

"I FEEL LIKE WE ARE WALKING INTO A TRAP, Daxen. We may cause people to be hurt."

"We do not cause any pain. This journey does not cause any pain. We are going to a source of water. We have always wanted to go to the well. The well has a nice story. The man was a common hero. And the spring was his special place."

"But others have turned this to prophecy. How do they know about our trips, tell the world where we will be going moments before we leave?" Anike asked.

"I have no idea. A spy?"

Anike shrugged. "No spies here."

"There was a list a long time ago, on our website. But we took it down," Daxen said.

"And our trips? Are they in the same order as they were listed on the site?"

"Yes. I believe so."

"That must be the source. They must have copied it."

"Time travel perhaps."

"Seriously, Daxen. This gives me the freak."

"So what. A guy in Uruguay announces we will be visiting some waters. People in Indonesia pray we have a safe journey. We do. No harm."

"But they have written all that stuff about how once we have visited the 'seven waters' then any action to achieve a goal is warranted. It is a time of action. Which means violence."

"We are not responsible for that, for the people in Indonesia. The followers."

"They are not our followers, Daxen. You said we were never to use that term. We must keep a distance."

"Father Duffy's Well was never posted as a destination. There were only six journeys planned in the early years. We stole the idea of the well, the story of the well, from the walkers – the Spanish Caminatorres, from Madrid. Father Duffy was a walker, more than a saint with holy waters."

"It was never posted? You sure?"

"Yes. We stole it from the Caminatorres. They came here 5 years ago. My cousin is married to one of them, a dentist. They walk everywhere. Father Duffy is like some kind of native savage saint to them. A robed Robin Hood who simply walked for justice."

He pulled out his phone and retrieved a map.

"He was a parish priest, appointed by a Bishop Fleming, and he had to walk back and forth between St. Mary's Bay and St. John's, to go to court. He built a church where a fish merchant did not like. Riot on the beach. Arrests. Charges laid. And he had to go to court, in St. John's."

"Father Duffy would walk to town, his case would get delayed. He'd walk back. Then it would happen again and again. They say he walked over 1500 miles, back and forth, and was finally acquitted."

"Well, how did they know, the Uruguayans?"

"I have no idea. It is a mystery."

"WOLF-CLAN, I believe," said Sandra.

"You can trace your family back to the middle ages?" Luke asked. The question was to both twins.

"Our father knows the stories," Sophie said. "Bishops. Kings. Battles. Great lands. Hangings."

"He would tell them to us when we were little," said Sandra, looking out the car window, uninterested.

"I wrote two school reports on our family history," Sophie continued. "One teacher, the guy from Kentucky, said I had an active imagination."

Mark pointed out the front window. "Does any of this look familiar? Like Norway?"

"We grew up in Cincinnati, Mark. Never been to Norway," Sandra said in a southern drawl.

"I imagine it does. The rocks and things," Sophie said.

"Kind of bleak," Sandra said.

"How would dogs live out here? In this barren land?" Sophie asked.

"I have no idea," Luke said.

"Anyway, I am glad my doctor cancelled and we could join you."

"Female doctor, in the Square?" Mark asked. He checked the interior rearview mirror.

"That's private, Mark. But yes. How do you know? That's creepy."

"Few good doctors in town. She is popular," Mark said. "My sister sees her."

"Very popular," said Luke.

"She's fucking Luke's cousin, the guy who runs the café," Mark said.

Sophie screwed up her face. The talk was a bit frank.

Mark looked in the rearview at Sophie.

"She was fucking Luke's cousin's uncle. But that ended. Cops were involved," said Mark, with spice.

"What kind of doctor is she?" Luke asked.

"A family doctor, obviously," Sandra said dryly, turning her head.

They all laughed. Luke almost burst a vein in his neck.

"Well I'm glad you could join us," Mark said.

"Tomorrow was out," Sandra said.

"She's going to see the Vagina Monologues," Sophie said.

"I'm waiting for the scary sequel, the Vagina Dialogues," Mark said.

After short consideration, Sandra laughed.

"There's a guy on Empire Avenue who calls himself 'The Vagina Whisperer'" Luke threw out.

Sophie laughed, blushing.

"Has Rabbittown under his spell does he?" Mark asked.

Sandra cycled her legs, giggling.

Luke placed two fingers on the inside of Sophie's forearm.

"He has on a tattoo on his left arm. *'Where there's feeling, there's hope'*, it says," Luke said, running his fingers from Sophie's elbow to her wrist. She relaxed.

"Wrong font, bad kerning, it runs to part of his hand." His fingers tapped the butt of the Sophie's palm. *"ope."*

She tittered.

Sandra turned in her seat and winked at her sister.

"You dogs," she said.

Sophie folded her arms.

"Dogs. Our mission today. Not sure if we'll see any dogs. But there have been sightings," Mark said.

"Why would people abandon their pets?" Sophie asked.

"Cruel, cruel people," Sandra echoed.

"Not sure. They leave them by the overpass to the Witless Bay Line, supposedly, and go back to town," Mark said.

"Or they take them camping in Butterpot Park, and leave them in the woods," Luke said.

"I can't imagine," Sophie said. There was a hint of Newfoundland in the way she said it.

Sandra looked out the window. No sign of buildings anywhere; all trees, ponds, and rolling hills of bare rock.

"God, there's nothing here," she said.

Mark looked back and forth from the rearview to the road.

"Don't look now, but I think we have some roadhead."

Sophie looked confused. Sandra turned and looked out the rear window of the four door pickup.

"In the sedan behind us?" she asked.

"Yes," Mark said. "Don't stare."

Sandra pretended to be giving something to her sister in the back seat. "I don't see it," she said.

"How could you see it?" Luke asked. "Let them pass."

"They have had plenty of chances. Autopilot," Mark said. "There. There she is."

Sandra squinted. "I see the woman. She... she dropped something." She returned to facing the front. "You're some bad," she said, tapping Mark lightly on his arm.

"Good driving is defensive driving," Mark said.

He pulled out and passed a large van bus, full of people wearing shades of green and grey. One had a green scarf with red trim.

Henry and June

THE SEDAN WAS QUIET. Having the radio on interfered with the telepathy, for beginners. Disagreement in musical tastes sealed the deal. Constable Henry Driscoll was driving, Sergeant June Fenwick the passenger.

Fenwick tried to be in the moment. She had better experience with Kelland doing the telepathic comms. She concentrated.

Fenwick – *This is a waste of time.*

Driscoll – *You need to pee?*

Fenwick – *This is a waste of time.*

Driscoll – *I agree. Just following orders.*

Fenwick – *It is a nice day.*

Driscoll – *I don't think we get extra pay.*

Fenwick double tapped her implant. It sent a direct signal to Driscoll informing him he was not 5 x 5, not loud and clear. Time to concentrate.

Driscoll rolled his hands around the steering wheel. This was hard – telepathy and driving. Besides, June Fenwick, well, she is undeniably hot, sexy, and she just mindfucks him all day, every day. It is unbearable. He imagined his brain was a taint of blue.

Frustrated, Fenwick removed her sunglasses and cleaned the lenses. She fumbled and dropped them on the floor of the car. She removed her seatbelt and reached down to retrieve them, at Driscoll's feet. She touched his leg slightly, so he knew where her hands were. Awareness is key.

Driscoll – *Roadhead!*

Fenwick – *What!!*

Fenwick sat up, glasses in hand. She cleaned them, slowly.

Driscoll – *That wasn't me.*

Fenwick put on her glasses. She stared at the handsome officer with the dirty mind.

Fenwick – *At ease, recruit. Concentrate.*

Driscoll- *Shit. The truck passed. We are directly behind.*

Fenwick – *From behind. Yes, baby.*

Driscoll tapped his implant twice.

Fenwick – *Faster.*

Driscoll – *We need to slow down. Should have a screen between us and the subject.*

Fenwick – *Scream. Depends.*

Driscoll – *Oh God.*

Fenwick – *Slow down. S – L – O – W.*

Driscoll – *We are okay. Our cover is not blown.*

Fenwick – *What is it when the sound of a word imitates the action of the word?*

Driscoll – *Longest transmission ever. Tuned in.*

Fenwick – *the word?*

Driscoll – *Onomatopoeia.*

Fenwick mouthed the word 'blowjob': an expulsion of air pushed by puckered lips; then a quick release, a retraction showing teeth, smacking lips, ending with a pop.

Driscoll had to shut his eyes. He had to shut down one of his senses. Dangerous while driving.

Fenwick – *Watch the road ahead.*

The police radio lit up. A voice said, "Operation Killick. All units. Muster at the well. Code Red. Subject is believed to be hot."

Fenwick spoke. "Back the fuck away from them. They have a bomb on board."

From discarded analog device, Ferryland colony

Messages

[There is a strong indication these events were simultaneous.]

Convergence

THE VAN WAS ON THE MAIN ROAD heading towards Father Duffy's Well, past Salmonier, in the center of the Avalon.

"Are we close Leonard?" one of the passengers asked.

"Yes. A few minutes."

"If you applied your power of observation to current conditions, how would you apply the five per cent principle," asked Niall Burnett, in the passenger seat.

"Not sure," replied Leonard. "Off the record, there is a great, untapped market for infused butters."

"How do you mean? Butter from peanuts?"

"Partially. Take salt. There should be five distinct grades of salted butter. There's Garlic, Dill, and Anchovy. But these are not celebrated, explored. Ginger butter, Curried butters, butter swissed with full tubes of chives, Lemon butters for seafood. Jesus, I'm hungry."

News came on the radio.

"A CONSTITUTIONAL CRISIS CONTINUES IN CANADA'S LARGEST PROVINCIAL DEMOCRACY.

MORE ALLEGATIONS SURFACED TODAY ON THE SCANDAL SURROUNDING THE ONTARIO PROVINCIAL ELECTION, STILL NOT RESOLVED THREE DAYS AFTER POLLS CLOSED. THE CHINESE MILITARY IS SUSPECTED TO HAVE HACKED INTO THE SERVERS STORING THE VOTES, AND ALTERING THE RESULTS.

243

AT THIS MOMENT, AMONG THOSE ELECTED TO THE ONTARIO LEGISLATURE STANDS: THREE HEADS OF CABBAGE, FOUR VARIETIES OF TURNIPS HOLDING DOWN 23 SEATS IN GREATER TORONTO RIDINGS; AND OTTAWA IS IN THE CONTROL OF THE DISCARDED EXERCISE EQUIPMENT PARTY.

THE BALANCE OF POWER SITS WITH AN ABANDONED '69 CUTLASS, OUTSIDE THUNDER BAY.

MORE ON THIS STORY... "

The broadcast broke into a Korean pop song.

Leonard snapped off the radio.

"We have company. Police are following us."

Niall Burnett raised his phone, fumbling for the video.

Three police cars were speeding up the road behind them. An unmarked sedan, with a magnetic cherry light propped on the roof, was keeping up with the police cruisers.

"That sedan has been trailing us since Butterpot Park," Leonard said.

The van came around the turn before the well. The road past was blocked off by two police cars. A policeman directed the van into the small parking area, directly off the main road.

Leonard parked the van and put up his hands. A policeman approached. Leonard rolled down the window.

"We have to ask you to put the van in park. Leave it running. Get out of the van and follow the officers." The policeman waved and several other officers raced in behind him. "Leave it running. It is important."

Leonard was shocked. "Just get out and follow you. Leave it running," he repeated.

Through Leonard's open window the police officer reiterated the same instructions in perfect German to the passengers. They reacted promptly, automatically, and all hands were soon out and around the bend, behind the increasing number of police cars in the area.

A senior police officer approached Leonard and pulled him aside. "Mr Livingstone, we have reason to believe an incendiary device has been planted on your vehicle. We will investigate, thor-oughly. The bomb squad will be set up shortly."

"I don't think I am insured. For bombs I mean," Leonard said nervously.

"Very few people are," the officer clipped.

A half hour passed before the bomb unit had the small robot set up. It looked like an aggressive industrial vacuum.

Niall Burnett's camera had run out of juice. He sulked in a ditch.

Leonard had a chance to show the Germans the well, from a distance, framed by two police cars. It was a simple fountain, a pipe sticking out of a wall in a small archway. Grotto minimalesque in the true Newfoundland tradition. The water spilled out into a trench edged by flatstones. The central stone hearth was embedded into a long low concrete wall.

A heated argument broke out amongst the Germans. Leonard thought it might be some kind of withdrawal, from their journey, or from his additives, he was not sure.

A special wall was set up, designed for protecting the command post. It quickly became a place for the senior officers to smoke out of the wind.

A couple of plainclothes officers, Fenwick and Driscoll, suited up in heavy gear. The robot was wheeled out.

Fenwick – *Position the 'bot. Park it. Let's use the mirror on the stick first.*

Driscoll – *Let the robot hold the fucking mirror.*

Fenwick – *It is a 12 foot pole, dumbass.*

Driscoll – *You hold the stick.*

Fenwick – *No problem.*

The robot stopped moving, square to the side of the van. Fenwick and Driscoll formed a tight unit, Driscoll hoisting a barrier shield and Fenwick grasping a long stick with a mirror taped on the end. It looked like a giant dental tool.

Driscoll spoke. "I'm getting feedback. Fuck. You?"

Fenwick spoke. "No."

She stepped outside the protection of the barrier, away from Driscoll, and extended the stick under the van.

Driscoll – *That's better. The howling is gone.*

Fenwick passed the mirror beneath the van, walking around the perimeter. She stopped near the rear. She raised her hand, making a fist and then extending her fingers, indicating she had found the bomb.

The officers behind the protective wall butted their cigarettes.

Driscoll – *Bomb?*

Fenwick – *Maybe. Yes. Damn.*

Driscoll – *What's the problem?*

Fenwick – *There's no clock.*

Driscoll – *What?*

Fenwick scrunched down for a better view at the mirror.

Fenwick – *There's no clock. Or countdown device.*

All the onlookers started to make serious effort to get away from the scene.

Driscoll – *Longer pole?*

Fenwick – *Shit, we are live. Think. What could be the trigger?*

Driscoll – *Cell phone?*

Fenwick – *No.*

Driscoll - *Wire to transmission? GPS?*

Fenwick – *No. No.*

Driscoll – *Massage?*

Fenwick – *Yes. But not now. Fuck the robot.*

A hoot came from the officers deep behind the line of cars.

Fenwick turned to look back at the senior officers. One was making frantic signals for them to return. She moved behind the protective barrier with Driscoll. He was in obvious pain.

"Sounds like dogs howling," he spoke.

They backed away slowly from the van.

In the complete silence they could hear the quadcopter, now almost overhead. Some officers pulled out revolvers and took aim at the drone. A small airhorn was dangling beneath the flying machine.

Fenwick – *Sound activated. Shit.*

An officer fired at the hovering device. The airhorn blasted.

The van exploded, the rear lifting four or five feet. Then, with a louder crack, the van spit in two. The fireball from the gas tank propelled Fenwick and Driscoll into parked vehicles. The central mass of the van came down on top of the well with a thud.

"Missed," was the body of a text message.

"Have great footage," quickly followed.

Father Duffy's Well. From Beth's Camera

Dogs

"It's LIKE A CHESSBOARD, or something. Giant pieces tipped over. Giant chess," Sandra said.

"Dropped from the bottom of glaciers. Rolled on by glaciers, a long time ago," Luke said.

They were on the barrens at the end of the park. The high ground was a blanket of solid rock, creased and curved in long arches, salted with discarded stones and boulders. Some crevices allowed for small ponds, small bodies of water. Tight moss anchored where it could.

"How do we get over there?" Sophie asked, pointing to a group off in the distance, bearing flashlights.

"Follow me," said Mark.

The four of them walked around a pond and through a passage between low bushes.

The group were the dog owners, carrying small bags of dog food and familiar toys, hoping to encounter their former pets.

A silver tipped fox slipped into the brush and let the party pass. A white owl perched on the highest rock.

They joined the group, assembled behind three large stones providing a prop for concealment.

Members of the group went out to the middle of the adjacent barren, before the wood of the park, and laid out piles of dog food, in familiar dishes. Many placed dog toys on the ground midway between the food and the rocks they would stand behind.

Shortly after the convoy was finished their baiting, right at sunset, a fox marched out into the barren, sniffing at the piles of food. It settled for a larger pile, nearer the center.

The fox chewed quickly, trying to keep his eyes wide open. It turned as it chewed, to cover greater range, the silver tail close to the ground.

Lightning sparked over the distant ocean.

After the distant thunder, a black mastiff charged out of the wood, growling like it was tearing the head off a devil as it ran. The fox shit on the ground, jumping six or seven feet. When it landed, it bounced in a different direction, and scrambled into brush.

The dog ran past the line of food, and snapped at the audience, able to mark a large territory with the threat of the snarl.

Sandra grabbed Mark's arm. "His eyes. Wild eyes."

The dog turned its back to the spectators and sniffed around. It settled on a large pile and started to slowly pick up the treats in its great mouth. It raised its head, and looked at the owl.

From the darkness many mongrels sauntered out, peacefully, fearless. Some fed; others wandered and sniffed.

One, a beagle, walked towards the rocks, tentatively, towards a lady's leather boot.

"Snoops!" an elderly man piped. "Snoops!"

There was a unity in the motion of all the dogs, set by the temper of the large mastiff. Their tails wagged in the same pattern, with similar tempos; their shoulders hunched and tensed in equal measure.

Sophie was in awe. This was the wildest thing she had ever seen.

All the dogs froze on cue, their ears and heads snapping to the west. They all cowered.

The owl left his perch and started gliding to the ground.

A loud distant percussive explosion came from the west, two loud cracks. The sound passed past.

The dogs continued eating, faster.

The owl lifted the beagle into the air, one talon ahold of a leg, the other, the tail. The dog yelped, twisted, and fell. It hit the ground, extinguished of life.

The dog pack retreated into the woods, receding from the wild cries of the people on the dark barren, without food.

The great owl soared silently towards the ocean.

Fragment from bone slice

LIGHT WAS STILL VISIBLE on the peaks of distant thunderheads over the ocean. The flat bottoms of the clouds darkened the water below. The path along the river, at the back of the properties running up the valley, was bathed in half-light. Michelle was used to the old trail, having travelled it frequently her whole life.

She stepped over the stones, went around the fences, and crossed the fields on her way to Beth's property, where the group was meeting, the latest incantation of the 'Girl's Club'. She had been an occasional participant years ago, when the goal was some good girl talk and salacious gossip; but she stepped away when it started to get seriously whacked – potions and charms, group chants and writhing; and, of course, drumming. The Girls Club, in these recent times, may have matured and subdued, providing an exchange for the cures for arthritic pain and menstrual cramps, but it also seemed on the verge of full blown lunacy.

It was bound to be fun. Old friends.

Michelle heard the slow beat of the drum as she made her way through the bush to reach the clearing well back on Beth's property. The clearing had a stone wall to the north and along the river side. On the south side of the clearing there was a large stone sauna, or sweat lodge, with a great view of the southern sky. The east was thick brush, separating the sunken clearing from the meadow behind Beth's house.

Beth's grandfather build the sauna for the enjoyment of his wife; she suffered from debilitating migraines and joint pain. A Danish seaman, a boarder with the family, suggested the cure, and helped in the building.

The site presented the two men with obvious anchors, foundation elements, for the sauna. An odd ridge of rock formed part of the southern border for the property. It stopped abruptly, with a gap about 15 feet wide, with a height of eight feet at the front edge of the ridge, sloping down to a three foot rise in the small clearing.

This ridge was made of dense rock, a single nub of a much greater, ancient, recent part of the base mantle of the earth. It appeared as a single pour, snaking back into the ground on the other side of the bramble brush, through brackish ground. It looked like the tip of a massive pool cue, greatly overgrown and forcing its way out of the earth, with slow determinism.

The active stick allusion was triggered by the stone directly in its path, fifteen feet past the end of the ridge, past the tip of the imagined stick, next to the meandering line of the river. The stone was round, a relaxed round, and slightly higher than the ridge. The slumping boulder had distinctive light density and colour. Compared to the iron rich red-black of the ridge, the lone rock also appeared to consist of a single material, white, translucent and finely porous; the collected sand and grit compacted by a long gone glacier grinding proto skeletons on the pool table of the mantle still nearby.

On the back line, near the middle of the gap between ridge and stone, the ground dipped again, creating a natural turret before the enclosed meadow.

The men used the turret as the body of a large hearth. From ridge to rock they ran a cord of apple-sized beach rocks. These were covered in slate, with a slate vertical wall for the low interior back wall. The rock wall curved into the angled roof, a loose laminate of slate, held by pillars of stone shaped like bones. The front wall was thick. Three interlocking layers of laid stone, with a low arched port, framed the southern wall.

Sitting inside, looking out the arch, you can only see the sky. Imprints of fossils, on the surface of the slate, shimmer in the light.

Fire in the hearth heated the lines of beach rocks, and the interior soon warmed. Moss on the roof released water, providing a consistent agent to the heating of the beach rocks at the base. It took a half days burning to get the sauna up to steam, so to speak.

It was quite the spot.

The young Danish seaman seduced the planter's young daughter, Beth's mother, in the sauna he helped build. He then skedaddled to St. Pierre and made sail for Venezuela, on a banana boat.

Beth's mother, as a young girl, thought she was making love to a Norse god, and would have a child of steel.

Instead she had Beth. Beth, perhaps the singularly best example for a life misled, fopping around like a walrus from life goal to life goal. Driven by ambition, she never travelled far. She has always lived in the house on this land. With her mother.

Beth had no good reason to leave, her mother reminded her a few times a day. The path of least resistance was to have no path at all; a simple enough plan for the likes of Beth.

She had a lot of time on her hands. And a perfect spot for a meeting of witches; at the end of the field, beyond the brambles, a sunken theatre of stone and thick wood.

The flatstone in front of the hearth was large enough for a group of 13 to congregate, standing, in a circle or in small assembly. The fire was a good setting, and the sauna encouraged naked opportunities.

She had her own ideas of how it could all work. Not there yet. Close, with some successes. Her coveted coven, of her own creation. The largest group she has ever had, before last Midsummers, was eight. And most of them just wanted to get drunk and bitch and complain, telling stories and swapping gossip.

When the real bone fide lesbians showed up last Midsummer, one of them wearing Leonard Livingstone's overalls, Beth hatched a plan. The goal was to get the lesbians naked. Make sure there's the spirit of a spell having been cast. And make sure she does not have another full circle of the sun before she enjoys the intimate company of a woman; any woman who doesn't tell her she need not go far.

That's how Leonard's crotch, the crotch from his workpants, ended up stuffed in the rocks of Manchu Pichu. It was an important part of the original spell Beth dreamed up, spontaneously. After a few vodka and sevens she sided up to the kinky-haired one and spun a tale of how Leonard was a threat to women of their kind. He couldn't help it. It was in the earth, where he lived.

Where he lived was the site of a pre-Cabot altar of death, she said, assembled by a Spanish captain, there to trade with the Basque. The harbour was the captain's place to sit and wait for the Basque to come by. The price for the whale oil was very dependent on the difference in the size of the cannons fashioned by the traders. And speed.

The Spanish captain would pick up some women in Marseilles and take them on the voyage across the Atlantic for the pleasure of the crew. It kept the men attentive, combative. But by the time they crossed, and had to park and wait, the situation was too explosive. He arranged for the ship's priest to declare the women as witches. He then converted the men, and they demanded the spectacle of burning.

They built a sunken flatstone track on a high clearing and drove stakes in the ground. They tied the woman to the stakes and burned them alive.

The natives who, from a safe distance, witnessed the many burnings over the years, the local clan known as the fog-dwellers, passed news of the event across the island. The chief, and two of the knowledgeable men, travelled to the mountains in the west on a mission to share the news of the barbaric menfolk who lived on the sea. The quest was successful. In following springs, the fog-dwellers would receive a message of the Basques first departure from the sandy beach, laden with whale oil. The message travelled from what is now called the Labrador coast to Quidi Vidi, along moments of trade.

The barbarians would soon be back.

Years ago, one of the witch women had escaped. She was Michelle's ancestor, the one with the strawberry hair.

Beth said Leonard's property was a place of evil. A place in combat with this hearth, her hearth, the good hearth. She leaned her hand into the kinky haired ones crotch, the heel of her hand pressing on the kinky haired ones' pubis, and said "We need to cast a spell."

Such a night changed Beth's life. She came up with new plans. The one that stuck was flying to Manchu Pichu, getting the ancient spirits, the ones who might have an issue with the Spanish, involved. She left her mother for 17 days, the best 17 days of her life.

Michelle emerged from the bush and handed Beth a bottle of pear brandy.

Beth welcomed her lifelong friend with a well-worn hug. Three flashes of lightning lit the valley, with several more on the Torbay headland. Beth and Michelle held each other till the thunder stopped.

"Nothing to worry about Michelle. Your sweetheart is safe," she whispered into Michelle's ear, smelling her hair. It smelled of fog and field.

"Good to hear," said Michelle. "Happy St. John's Day, sister."

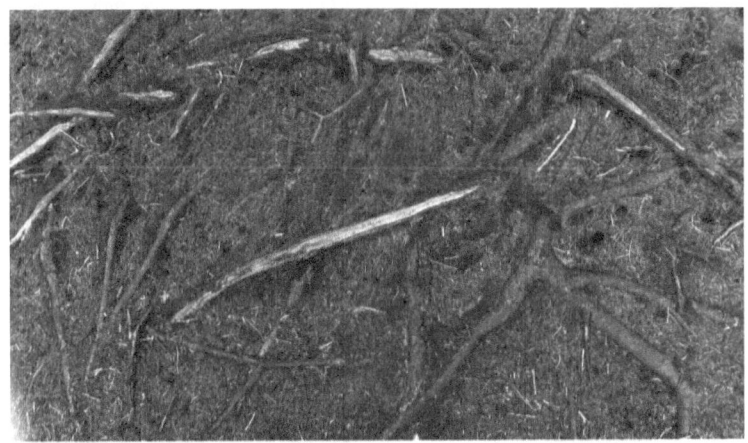

From Beth's camera.

Found in area known to have been location of colony claim

Found on Luke's phone

Defining Moments – Diane

[Anchor event.]

Over Exposure

I F IT WASN'T FOR THE CURRLAX from Notre Dame Bay, Diane would never had been on TV, as far as she was concerned. A localized variant on gravlax, the Norwegian recipe of salmon cured in salt, sugar and dill, currlax was comprised of fresh salmon wrapped in a slurry of curry, cranberry juice and whole blueberries, smoked in a peat moss oven. It was food candy. You could literally feel your body rebuilding itself with every bite. The salmon melted in your mouth, the smell hitting the brain by osmosis, especially paired with the right white wine, or pear cider.

She had three boxes of the new delicacy and she distributed one freely amongst her regulars. She must have impressed the right people at the right time, because two months later the Logy Fresh story was all over the lifestyle media. Airplane magazines, glossies for those with restaurant gas ovens and built-in steam butlers, all craved a local story with feel-good points. Everyone wanted to read about fresh, specialized foods, with outrageous health benefits, supporting dozens of dedicated artisans entrepenuering their way to success. The burlap, ribbons and mason jars reflected well on the Connemara Irish marble in the accompanying photographs.

Local celebrities claimed to use the service, and everyone wanted to sign up. Diane asked young Bud if he could help with the requests, and he did. They decided to cut off the customer list after it had doubled. The local media desperately wanted to do stories on Logy Fresh, but Diane refused. It would be bad for business, others would walk the trail she and Leonard has cut.

She went to Toronto to get some supplies, and visit her friend Katherine. She hoped to source sprouts for African pepper plants, Grains of Paradise and kaffir lime. Bud had set up the greenhouse and was doing some pretty exotic botanical experiments. He fixed it up and brought in new grow lamps. He had three grades of fortified grow medium, and a watering system channelled through a slew of fish. The kid just took to it.

The trip was planned before all the media attention. The jaunt to Toronto in the spring was a regular break, and Katherine was an old friend. Katherine had been hooked up with a media producer for the national broadcaster. Diane was happy for Katherine and all, but she figured Michael blew into St. John's, learned his chops doing productions on the local music scene, and bounced back to Toronto, taking Katherine with him. They lasted seven or eight years, but Katherine had a child fathered by someone other than Michael, and the relationship ended bluntly. Luckily for Katherine the father was a personality, and all that was politely handled. She was cared for in opportunity as much as anything else. She became an editor, which is a kind of professional friend; a confidant in the media world centered in the Big Smoke.

Michael's response was to have more elaborate facial hair, and a rearrangement of tattoos and jewelry.

Katherine took Diane to a party. A media party, easy to like. Everyone was so well dressed there was bound to be a lot of flirting. The room sparkled with familiar faces, large shiny heads on slight, suitable bodies. Loud polite laughter, starched collars and war heels were three constants across the black garbed guests.

A political columnist for a national paper honed in on her, and a TV researcher saved her.

She gets introduced, and is quickly invited to sit as a guest expert on a panel discussing locavores on national television. She has skin that glows under studio lights. Her smile and enthusiasm beamed. She even made the host look good.

So, she does great. Her piece is recycled on other news programs, featured on the broadcaster's internet offering and is extremely popular as a standalone video, posted by pirates.

Without Leonard she is sad. She calls him.

She said she realized if she wasn't at the party she would not have had the opportunity to be presented as an expert in her field. They never would have talked to someone in St. John's when someone in Toronto was handy. She was economically available.

"I'm have to hang up Len. My eyes. Does everything turn into a grind? Fuck Toronto. Really, I have to sleep"

Diane hangs up and lies on her bed. The room is spinning. She reaches under her housecoat to feel her heart. She finds a lump on her breast.

Livingstone Homestead - original

and

Inversion capture (sub 50kz) from above image - noisy
background

Apéritif

L EONARD WAS IN THE KITCHEN preparing apéritifs when he heard the low groans and acute yelps out back. Bud, Colleen, and Michelle were on the patio, waiting for a BrainSugar. Niall, and Colleen's guest, Jean, were seated at the table, politely waiting for everyone to be served.

❖ BrainSugar: one shot Absente, one shot ice cold water, one shot ice cold Cranberry Juice. When drinking, top off w CJ.

From the kitchen window Leonard could see Daxen in the corner of the garden coming out of the pathway that led to the firepit. He was bent like a paper clip, his splayed legs pushing him forward. He was punching himself in the hips, which seemed to cause relief.

Anike ran out behind him, topless, with one arm still in her thin cashmere top.

Leonard downed the two drinks he had prepared and made his way to the yard.

Daxen was yelling to Anike to get some ice and open the 'goddamn' sauna. He was on his knees, bent over, screaming through his own white noise.

"What seems to be the problem?" Leonard said.

Anike turned to him and shrugged her shoulders.

"The problem," Daxen screamed, "is your Blueberry compote flavoured with 'Goulds Chili Peppers'. What the fanny are in those chili peppers?" With that, he fell to the ground, openly crying.

"St. Francis Blueberries, cooked in spices, featuring hothouse chilies from the Goulds," he said.

Daxen grunted. He was not satisfied.

"The greenhouse is actually in Kilbride. The Goulds, somehow, sounds tastier," Leonard said. "The exact spices are a secret."

Daxen went wide-eyed, succumbing to shock.

"I'll share. If you'd like. If you think it will make you feel better."

Leonard was puzzled. Anike turned to him and made an 'O" shape with her mouth. She then barbed her tongue against her cheek, in a repetitive motion, followed by a shrug of her bare shoulders

"You," Leonard said, "and Daxen were down the path..." he trailed off.

"Friction," Daxen announced. "I thought it was friction. But those peppers in Annie's mouth, were digging in, like piranha." He drooled.

Leonard let out a laugh. He yelled to Bud to stoke the sauna. He asked Michelle to get Daxen a BrainSugar, a few pain reliever pills, and lots of ice.

Anike leaned into Leonard, laughing. He placed a hand on her bare shoulder.

Daxen stood up, grasping his crotch, and made for the sauna like he was in a sack race, without the sack, but holding his own as everyone tried not to laugh.

Leonard never took his hand off Anike's bare shoulder. It felt like a balustrade to the here and now. He felt if he let go, he would tumble.

Anike leaned away from him, after Daxen. Leonard stood, falling gracefully. He bent his knees for the landing, preparing for the turn.

From Jean's camera - Livingstone Homestead

Found on Jean's camera

still....

[Key event. This event aligns the previous stories. Murphy cluster redacted.]

THE COMMOTION SETTLED and everyone returned to relaxing: watching gulls dive and wheel over the cliffs; reading books; checking the vegetable garden; drinking tall glasses of ice water.

"This place needs a dog," Leonard said to Michelle.

"Get a real dog," Michelle replied.

She was standing in the patio door, half in shadow.

Leonard had scallops braising on the barbeque. He was going to set each of them with a necklace of sweetly vinegared capers, on porous hardbread cured in honey, crowned with heavily peppered slivers of carrot.

He paused to admire the line between dark and light running up Michelle's legs and torso.

"Smells good, Leonard," she said, her knees indicating a shift.

Niall, standing inside the sunken root cellar, the upper half of his body sticking out of the door in the cellar's roof, bobbed up and down on his toes, his hands in his pockets, his hair dancing around his head in the wind.

Jean was taking pictures.

"You look like a statue on Easter Island," she said.

A large dog leaped out of the woods of the lower garden. The dog had a golden shock through its forequarters, woven into its shiny black torso and legs. It looked like it was running the colour right off his body as it moved. The dog was the strongest, fiercest and friendliest form of life Leonard had ever seen.

267

The dog hit the ground once, and bound, high, for Jean's back.

In the blink of an eye, the blue sky turned bright white, bathing everything in soft light.

Daxen saw the daytime moon emerge from the fading flash, reflecting the sun of the earth.

The light lifted, paused at the edge of the atmosphere, and departed. The dark moved in.

The ground dropped under Leonard's feet, slightly. He fell to his knees, into Michelle. Bud fell down mid-step. The Germans were ground surfing, the world shifting beneath them.

Down. Down. Up. Back down. Up.... Up.

Reality was having jump cuts, without sound.

The ground shot to the side, like someone pulling on a carpet, tugging it to make it square, and not getting it right.

Michelle screamed into Leonard's chest.

The air moved. It shot a wind so slight in its profile Leonard could feel it tear over his head as if he was being scanned. By the time the air was rushing past his ears, his nose was back in the calm. His lungs hurt. Holes in his eardrums snapped with the shock.

The compacted atmosphere crystalized. Cracks of light rose from the ground into a sky losing colour.

Leonard lifted Michelle. Her hair was spiked straight out. Her eyes shut. Her lips slightly parted. Light was bubbling out of her mouth. She felt delicate.

She kissed him.

Earth. Leonard could smell fresh earth.

The horizon was a thin, deep, black line. The ocean roared.

Something grabbed Leonard by the strap of his overalls and dragged him for several feet before tossing him and Michelle into the root cellar, their bodies getting stuck in the doorway before they fell to the flatstone floor below. They were next to Colleen, who was laying aside Niall and Jean. Leonard remembered a hopeful letter he had written to a girl he met at Wasaga Beach when he was 14. Daxen fell in the doorway, his arms outstretched. Michelle reached up for him. Anike came tumbling in over Daxen, and then he was pushed down into the space by Bud, who closed the door to the underground storage space behind him.

"The others," Bud panted in the dark, "are dead. They exploded. Their lungs blew apart. Blew their bodies apart."

Leonard was sad they never had a chance to try his scallops.

Bud opened his mobile phone to have some light. It was no longer an electronic device, just cleverly arranged minerals and metals.

The earthen room was filled with the sound of a wet, sharp howl of a dog. It seemed to lessen the shake.

Niall stood and wedged the door open with his shoulder. The animal stepped into the root cellar and sat at his feet.

Leonard flicked a wooden match.

The air smelled of charcoal. The flame went thin.

He took a small mirror from inside his coat and reflected the flickering flame.

The air changed into orbits of intense light. Leonard could see through Daxen, lying on top of him. He could see through the six feet of compacted dirt in the walls of the root cellar. He could see down into the ground, down through the crust to the small sun at the center of the earth, surrounded by water.

A horizon of fire ringed below a foggy sky of women on crucifixes.

The dog blocked the swirls of exploding light, his silhouette against the horizon, now black from sea to Mars. Within the outline Leonard saw something good.

The ground twisted as if set on a massive fine spring. There was so much noise there was nothing to hear.

Leonard may have passed out. He may have died.

The ground danced for three more days. The noise roared for five.

When Bud came out of the root cellar the ocean was gone.

The smell of furnace is still in the air.

My Closing Remarks

This collection is the best reconstruction of how people lived at the time of the Event. There is no indication of an awareness of lithospheric activity; no mention of any warning signs amongst this group, or any other. The people in the region of Arabia, where the land disappeared, have been lost to the belly of the earth and the newly formed seas. We may never know if they had warnings.

Ground zero was where the ground vanished, ceased to be.

The collapse of the Arabian plate has been the defining Event of our age. Our recovery is often measured against an imaginary degree of the health and happiness of the people living before this geoclasmic readjustment.

The current theory is the Arabian Plate, a keystone tectonic structure between Africa, Asia and Europe, rose suddenly, and having been released from opposing pressures, quickly collapsed to a point well below the levels of the surrounding seas; vanishing beneath the waters.

Geoiscists have theorized the lithographic keel beneath the Arabian plate was knocked by a large sublimation released from the African plate.

The lithographic keel of tectonic plates is a large root system grounding the continents deep into the mantle of the earth. Sublimations are where one plate goes underneath another, or, as in this case, the bottom layer of a continental mass peels away and collapses into the furnace of molten rock boiling beneath the plates.

The evidence suggests the rising and collapse of the Arabian Plate was finished in minutes. The standard model of understanding is if a rock is thrown 500 feet into the terrestrial air until the force of gravity draws it back, for a drop of 3 miles, this would be the amount of time for the initial change. Others have proposed there was a period of super gravity during the collapse.

Evidence suggests the European plate was not involved. After the sinking of Arabia, Europe was bridged to Africa through the land known as Italy. The Mediterranean Sea divided, and the eastern portion joined the newly formed Subterranean Sea, an extension of the Indian Ocean.

These subjects, on the eastern coast of North America, probably experienced a lower level of airborne debris than those inland. Trees, residential debris and large objects, such as airborne vehicles, had a significant impact on the survival rates of inland residents.

Image reconstructed from satellite transmissions.

The force of the event was enough to cause the debris ring around the Earth and the warbling of the orbit of the moon, where new colonies now exist.

Many other stories have been extracted from this cluster. They may be presented in alternate portfolios. The story of the Downtown Creative Collective's Summer Season is intriguing, entertaining and somewhat tragic. This suggests a much later date for the Event, which can be possible in the multiple storylines produced through Narrative Extraction. Dennis Livingstone's adventures as a man on the run in the Avalon Wilderness has produced a fascinating volume on the signs used by men on the barrens. Michelle's strands lead back into the story of her family, from the Breton shore, and many of the individuals in the area. Ed Kelly, heavily redacted in this run, has a rich, and somewhat comical, set of escapades leading to an independent form of governance, a state administered by lesbians. Bud's tales pick up a little over a year after the Event and have clean imprints, according to early narrative tests. It is an exciting account of survival and features many games played with decks of cards.

Impressions of the early natives, the fog-dwellers and their kin, are everywhere. They are constant, radiating through all possible narratives. Their legends are a guide to the interpretation of animal stories, which so far have proven impossible to chronicle, due to limiting temporal models.

There is a strong push to uncover the origins for sending machines into space with the hope of finding sanctuary. Extractions, such as the ones presented here, give a strong sense of the world these people wished to recreate. A world with limited insights into the future and tentative connections to the past; a world in which the individual could live a rich interior life while trudging through a rather mundane terrestrial existence; a world of companionship and caring, love and laughter; a world where loss was real, and forging ahead proved the victory.

There are great learnings to be made from such studies.

There has been significant recovery of the electromagnetic transmissions near this time. They seem excessively concerned with conflict, 'chase' scenes and a preoccupation with a continuance of the narrative methods presented by the Greeks: Stories of Kings and Queens, murder and mayhem, wars and mysterious gods. These derivatives are mixed with cartoons of bears selling toilet paper, elderly on-stair elevators, and sports heroes hawking hearing aids. This formula does not seem to have a direct relation to the audience, but rather acts as a simplification of the human experience for the creators and

m

minders of the act of storytelling. As well, they seem to have little or no relevance to the current efforts to revive a viable, happy, model for the emerging class of 'individuals', free to live a singular life, in a group setting.

Remember, feedback is essential in a system of communications, and the producer of this folio, The Institute of Narrative Reconstruction, encourages the exchange of impressions to build a greater understanding of those before us, so we may have common direction in the cycles ahead.

Project Lead: NF7717044

The Institute of Narrative Reconstruction

Atlas Colony,

Royal Navy Moon Base Umbria

Dated, E763

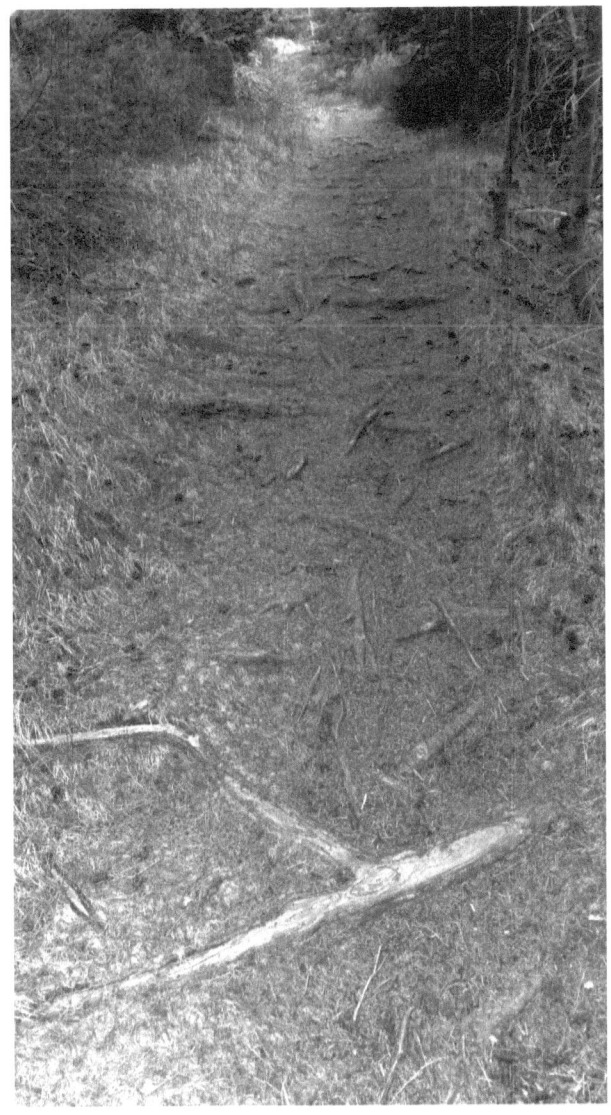

Standard deviation, Alpha channel - NF8528887

About the Author

Dave Roe is from St. John's, Newfoundland, Britain's oldest colony.

Dave programs collaborative computer systems, takes pictures, and he loves to cook.

Photo: Jean Roe

Dust Cover

What people are saying about Troubles in the Colony!

"Roe has wasted my time like no other."

- Eamonn Gilchrest, *Irish Economist Weekly*

"As messy as my father's shed. More convoluted than my sister's purity"

- Ginger Jacquir, *Bishops Fall Review*

"Ω∎⊘𝕞Γ◇◇"

- Amstrad PPC 512/640, *Goa Ecycling*

"Am I allowed to regift this?"

- Richard Richards XVI

"Of all the books I didn't read this year, I think Troubles was the most enjoyable, refreshing and life-changing, by far. A quick non-read."

- Everyone in Montreal

"Dad, where's my birth certificate. I need to check something,"

- Jean Roe, *Author's Child*